I0629479

EYES ON ME

KELCIE MARTIN

Copyright 2025 Kelcie Martin

Cowpokes Who Cry LLC

Pueblo, Colorado

All rights reserved. No portion of this book may be reproduced or transmitted in any form or by any means, electronic, mechanical, photocopying, recording, or otherwise, without express written permission of the author, except as permitted by U.S. copyright law. No generative artificial intelligence (AI) was used in the writing of this work. The author expressly prohibits any entity from using this publication to train AI technologies to generate text, including, without limitation, technologies capable of generating works in the same style or genre as this publication.

ISBN Paperback: 979-8-9875218-9-2

ISBN (ebook): 979-8-9928686-0-9

LCCN: 2025904869

www.cowpokeswhocry.com

Cover Design by Kateryna Vitkovska

Edited by Meg McIntyre at Phantom Pen Editorial

Proofread by Kaitlin Slowik at Kaitlin Slowik LLC

Interior design and formatting by Fox Formatting

To everyone who never felt like they belonged. Your purpose is much bigger than belonging. You were meant to stand out.

CHAPTER

ONE

A LONG GRAY NECK EXTENDED IN FRONT OF ME, PROVIDING A therapeutic distraction from my constant state of dread. The dark tones of the horse's form were bold against the dry yellow grass. Small whispers drifted from one blade to another. The quiet was especially eerie during the cool morning, a stark contrast to living in the city for the last eight years.

The appendage swayed back and forth, slowly regulating my nervous system exactly the way I needed. The only things visible between the ears of my horse were rolling hills and fat, happy cattle. The whispers of the land continued, reminding me that everything was OK.

Dad was shipping his steers off over the weekend, and I had a break in my clinicals. The last semester of medical school was testing the strength of my mental stability. The only thing standing between me and a mental breakdown was my twenty-year-old horse Scooby and his pretty grulla coat. It had started to gain its winter fluff, the dew accentuating the smoke-colored hair. His coal-black mane matched the color of what remained of my soul, the one I'd signed away to work in the medical field. His large stature was misleading; the sight of a jackrabbit made him flinch. Regardless, the 500 head of cattle didn't know that side of him. All they saw was a large animal with a human rider. That was their cue to get movin'.

"How's school, girl?" Dad belted. The cattle were moving away from the stock tank, groaning in unison. It was hard to hear, but he knew why I was there. I was having a hard time. The pressure of school was getting to me, and I wasn't sure if I would make it to the residency stage of my journey.

"I'm surviving, Dad. That's all I can do." I held back the frog in my throat as I spoke. I could feel it jumping around, hitting my uvula over and over again.

"Get 'er done, kid! You're so close," he shouted at me as we pushed the cattle east toward the house. I smiled, because for some reason he always made things seem much simpler than they were. Just finish. That's all I had to do. God, I wished it was that easy.

Dad sent me back west for about twenty head we'd missed in the corner of the pasture. I was grateful to leave because the frog had escaped and I had tears rolling down my face. How could I get almost eight years into this and be so God damn confused? I didn't want to be a doctor anymore. What would I do? Work on the ranch? How could I move back? Everyone I'd bad-mouthed from my small town would judge me. They would all know I couldn't hang with the big dogs in Denver.

The grass brushed against Scooby's legs, drawing my attention to the silence that settled when my mind wasn't racing. I stifled sniffles that left my nose irritated and plugged. The farther I got from the herd, the louder the quiet became.

I was supposed to do big things—make something of myself. Becoming a doctor meant helping people. It meant avoiding becoming my mother. I didn't want to fall into addiction. I didn't want to take down everyone in my path the way she had. The one person who I should have been able to depend on had left me. I wanted to be dependable for my dad, my patients, and my friends. I wanted to make something out of the heart she'd broken so many years ago.

The tears formed two rivers on my face, streaming down into the hoodie I was wearing. *God damnit.* No one knew the Colorado I was in. The busy streets of Denver could never be as uncomfortable with silence as the eastern plains could. Home was a place where you had to sit with your thoughts. The noise that usually influenced decisions was absent. Home was the ranch. Home was thirty miles from civilization, where the cows outnumbered the humans. Home was the only place I could think for myself without being drowned out by the expectations of society.

Scooby's hooves stamped impressions in the long blades of grass. I looked up, wondering if I'd lost the cattle in the gloomy fog that was still lifting. Shivering, I sniffled a few times, trying to gather myself. The tears started to clear, and I scanned the horizon for black figures in the distant corner of the fenced area.

Nothing.

Scooby's ears perked up, his skin trembling beneath my legs. Dad always said he would grow out of his skittish ways, but apparently not. There was nothing in front of us. My hands gripped the reins, ready for him to do a few crowhops across the pasture.

"Calm down, dude, nothing's there," I lectured. His hide shook violently over the muscle it protected.

His feet started to dance. He kicked up the wet dirt, unmasking an earthy smell. It was a long way down if I fell off, and a long walk home if I lost my horse. As his feet continued to dance, I heard a clanking.

"There must be some metal treasures out here, Scooby!"

My mood lightened when I realized we may have found a collectable trinket. Dad had kicked up old teapots and glass bottles from back in the day. Every chance he got, he hopped off his horse, surveying the land for old arrowheads or mementos the past had left behind. After all, we were part of the Wild West.

"Whoa, WHOA . . ." I said low and slow, attempting to calm him as I made my way down his large frame. I paused with one foot in the stirrup and the other leg on its way down to the ground.

When I trusted that Scooby wasn't going to run away with me, I jumped, landing on both feet at once.

Clank.

What the hell? It felt like I'd just landed on a large metal drum. I jumped up and down a few times, still holding the leather reins in my right hand. The dirt around me seemed disturbed, the vegetation turned over.

Clank, clank, clank. Scooby's hooves clanked behind me, hinting at something that seemed to be buried beneath the pasture. It definitely wasn't a small trinket.

"Oh God, Scooby, would ya chill out?" I argued with the horse who couldn't speak. He hummed in protest, raring against the reins.

"Hey, he—" My low tones were cut off by a rumble beneath my feet.

The reins were torn from my hand, leather ripped, burning my palm. Scooby leaped away from the moving object. The clods of mud began to slide, exposing a shiny silver treasure. I was two feet off the ground, and I could see Scooby running east. I froze before I could move, assessing the fastest way to the ground.

I followed Scooby's lead, my boots not gaining traction on the metal object hovering above the pasture. My arms pumped and my knees drove high, begging for some momentum to get me to the edge.

I was lifted higher. The object seemed to get longer and longer as I tried to escape to the ground.

"Fuck!" I shrieked. "DAAAAD!" I begged, knowing he was too far to hear me.

Clank, clank, clank, my boots slammed against the metal. The edge was so close. I had one more leap to go until . . .

I tripped. My foot smacked the raised light on the edge of the object, the heat burning through the leather of my boot. I grasped at the air as my back slammed against the edge of the vehicle. I had made it off the object, and the ground caught me. I was safe.

My ankle throbbed with pain. My blood moving against the newly burnt skin stung. At first, I thought I had stumbled upon a plane crash, but that was no plane. Two giant turbine engines carried a cylinder cockpit. There were no wings and no propellers. The vehicle hovered above me, taking the layer of pasture overtop with it. Clods of dirt fell into my mouth. Dirt blew into my face.

There was no time to clear the blinding dust particles from my eyes.

The sky above me was gloomy, full of nothing but atmosphere. Whatever I'd just fallen off of was gone.

CHAPTER

TWO

"Jess, did you hear anything I just said?" A voice underwater nagged at my internal monologue.

The less I slept, the harder it was to fake it. I couldn't get out of my head, and Angie wasn't really helping. She recognized my blank stare, the disassociating. You know, the ways I survived the day without crawling out of my own skin with overstimulation?

"Yeah, Ang, I just really haven't been sleeping," I managed to answer as the ambient noise around me became less muffled.

What she didn't know was what I'd seen two weeks ago. I was debating whether I needed to seek therapy, put myself in a psych ward, or maybe just run away to a remote city in the southern hemisphere and never come back. No one would suspect a thing. But telling her was the last thing I wanted to do. She was my best friend. And although she loved me for my weird personality, she for sure would have me put in a mental institution if I told her what happened. And if I was confined to an institution, *they* could easily find me there.

"I know it's been hard lately, but we can't quit now," Angie murmured as we both walked out of the hospital.

"I know you're trying to be positive right now, but I'd throw it all away for a forty-five-year-old neurosurgeon. Seven and a half years of school and all I have to show for it is crippling anxiety and a caffeine addiction." I was back in reality for the most part. At least, she thought I was. That was all that mattered.

"OK, Ms. 'I'm an independent woman. No man on this planet can give me the freedom of my own career,'" she said, mocking me. I think I'd said that four years ago, before the grueling days of med school.

"Fuck it. Hand me a mixer and call me Betty Crocker." I snorted at my own joke. She rolled her eyes, knowing I would rather die than have a man take care of me. We hopped in her used Toyota Camry. It was still kicking after our wild days in undergrad. The paint was fading and the carpet on the floor mat was a weird color of green where one of us had puked in the passenger seat. We swore we would never drink again after that night. Now look at us.

I had agreed to meet some friends at a brewery after our clinical rotations. Although I didn't need alcohol to add to my uneasiness, maybe it would push away the inner demons I was fighting. Were they demons? I didn't know. Should I go to church? Maybe. Instead, I'd drown the feelings in a stiff martini. I had come a long way from Burnett's vodka, whipped cream flavor, dumped into a Sonic slushie.

When we parked, I stepped onto the ledge of the sidewalk, my foot still aching from tripping at my parents' house. It reminded me of the incident I refused to acknowledge. Downtown Denver sang a tune that I realized I was now used to. The lights flashed as the sun went down and men in suits rushed to beat their commute back to the suburbs. Musicians lined the sidewalk, their brass instruments fighting against the noise of the traffic.

"Jess, Jesus Christ, you're doing it again. Can you at least blink and nod to pretend you're listening to me? The least you could do is keep me company." Angie was actually mad this time. If I didn't get my shit together, she was going to start asking questions.

"Gosh, I'm sorry. I'm a little messed up from the last patient we saw," I lied.

"The geriatric with bad feet? Yeah, OK, Jessica." She raised one eyebrow, wanting more.

"His dog was overweight because he couldn't walk him anymore. You know how I am about animals!" I was really too good at lying. She pretended to believe me for the time being, but the massive group of med students at the door of the brewery distracted her from questioning me further. The walk from our parking spot to the brewery had clearly not been long enough for me to gather myself.

"Jess, are you going to let me buy you one drink before we finish the semester? Look, I know your weird rules about men and their contributions to society. At least let me contribute one of those nasty martinis," Gabe boomed from across the bar. He had been trying to date me since we were in undergrad. He was still caught up on a one-time make out session in the laundry room of the old rental house Angie and I used to have.

"Filthy. I like them filthy. I want it to have so much olive juice my shoes won't fit tomorrow. I want to feel the salt expanding my cankles." Everyone giggled. Apparently, people thought I was funny.

Gabe handed me a dirty martini and the dry vermouth coated my mouth as soon as I took a sip. The insides of my cheeks started to sweat. I wasn't sure if I loved what I tasted or if I was going to throw up.

"You OK? I told them to make it how you like it. I even asked for the extra olives." Gabe stared at me.

"It's good. Long day," I replied, trying to ease his try-too-hard expectations. I really did feel bad. I wasn't trying to be mean, but my flashbacks were making me sick to my stomach, and I'd left my anxiety meds at home. The thought of passing out cold after taking a Xanax when I got home sounded like pure bliss.

The martinis kept coming. Eventually Gabe stopped ordering them for me when Angie whispered in his ear. My jokes weren't funny anymore. They were hurtful. I was projecting my own insecurities onto everyone else.

"Harold, you gonna pass out again in labor and delivery?" My voice carried across the room to my babysitters. I was in trouble with both of them. I slammed the last martini, tossed the olives to my molars, and started toward the door.

"Don't worry, Harold, maybe one day you won't be afraid of what a female's body can do. It's highly unlikely, though." I crushed all four of the olives, holding back the mouth sweats. Puking would admit defeat. Harold blushed, and I managed one more giggle before I was hit by the oxygen-depleted Denver air.

The Uber driver pulled up in a silver Tesla. I was supposed to be the designated driver, another reason Angie was mad at me.

"What the fuck am I doing wrong here?" I belted. I pointed at the car door, my arm flopping like a rubber chicken.

"Jess, come on, just get in. We're going home." Angie was being patient, but the liquor made me disregard my friend's calm nature.

"No, seriously. Why try? Eight years of stress and turmoil, and I still have the shitbox Ford Fuckin' Ranger Dad gave me. I don't have a heater and my—"

"We know, Jess, and your windows have a manual lever. And the world hates you, and med school sucks. And all you wanted to do is leave that shithole of a town. Can we just have a peaceful ride home?" Angie changed her tone. She was done with my shit.

My stomach turned and my head spun. After holding back puke the whole ride home, I made my way to the front door of our apartment. Angie didn't talk to me the entire time. I noticed her soft brown eyes begging for patience. I had tested her for so long; it was getting harder and harder for her to put up with me.

We both had brown eyes, but hers were different than mine. Hers carried warmth, forgiveness, and empathy. She pulled her bangs back as she unlocked the door. What had I done to deserve her as a friend?

The last thing I remembered was a Xanax and a tall glass of water sloshing around with the alcohol in my stomach. At three a.m., the alcohol started to wear off, and I could feel my foot aching again. I wanted to wake up, but I couldn't. I wanted to go back to sleep, but I couldn't do that either.

Instead, I tossed and turned, replaying different moments of my life. Images of school, late nights, and alcohol . . . High school, overachieving, feeling confused about where I fit in the world. My personality was torn between the ways of the city and the rural world I was raised in. There was a void I could never fill after I lost Mom. I never fit in, and when I did, it was because I was pretending. I was there to please people, to help people. I still didn't know what made me happy. I only knew that I didn't want to be a disappointment.

And now, I also had to convince myself that aliens weren't real.

THREE

ANGIE CAME INTO FOCUS THROUGH CRUSTED EYES. SHE FACED AWAY from me, waiting for me to get up. I contemplated pretending to be asleep until she had to leave for her yoga class, but she deserved more than that.

"Thanks for getting me home . . . again." That got her attention. She heard me but didn't bother to turn around.

"Ang?" I coaxed. I was treading lightly. I'd used up all of my chances with her, and she was not about to let me off that easy. There was the time I'd passed out under a booth at the bar and no one could find me. Or the time I cracked my head on concrete stumbling home, and I begged her to give me stitches instead of making me go into the ER. She'd covered me many times when I was late for class, or when I didn't pull my weight in group projects. I was basically her unruly toddler, except much bigger with a more creative vocabulary.

"Jess, let's cut the bullshit. You've been up for at least thirty minutes, and we all know you're avoiding the ass-chewing that's about to commence." She spoke to the floor.

The room was silent. She was right, and unfortunately, I

had nothing left to say. What could I say? *So, I went home and I think I saw an alien spaceship.* The morning light shone through my window. I followed the dust particles through the beam of light to her face. She contorted her expression, proving to me how mad she was. She held her own cup of coffee, and I could see mine, piping hot, sitting on the table in the corner of the room. No matter how hard she tried, she couldn't help but love me. I tried not to laugh at her angry look. It didn't suit her. I stared at the lines of her face, jealous that there seemed to be no damage from aging, stress, or excessive alcohol consumption. After she'd spent the last eight or so years taking care of me, I had no idea how she still looked so good. I waited for her to finish her ass-chewing. I owed her that much.

"Look, I'm worried about you. Ever since you went home, you've been acting weird. The last two weeks you've been all over the place—more than usual. You aren't engaging at the hospital. I have to cover for you all the time because you're lost in another dimension—"

"You got that right," I murmured under my breath.

"Jess! Come on!" she lectured.

"I know, I know! I'm sorry. I wish I could explain where my head's at, but I just don't even know where to start." I could tell her guard was starting to come down.

"And the drinking . . . It's getting out of control too. We aren't young and dumb anymore, or at least we can't use that as an excuse now that we're almost done with med school. The real world is about to give us both a slap in the face, and I can't do it without my best friend. OK?" Her desperation was the only thing that kept me from deflecting the conversation with sarcasm.

I nodded.

"I can't either." I lifted one corner of my mouth, waiting for her to drop the angry façade. I was in the clear for now, but I had some serious demons—or extraterrestrials—that I needed to deal with.

Angie and I had met in our freshman year of undergrad. We were both from small towns on opposite sides of the state, both raised in a single-parent household. The pressure to succeed was something we were all too familiar with. All we wanted to do was show our parents how much we appreciated them, that all of their hard work raising us wasn't for nothing. We wanted to find purpose and heal our abandonment issues. Each of us had watched one parent leave, and we blamed ourselves for that. We wanted to feel needed, appreciated, and like we belonged somewhere.

Angie never met her dad. He left after she was born. And my mom? She decided to get behind the wheel drunk when I was seven years old. I remembered her, but even at a young age, I resented the fact that the bottle meant more to her than her family. After the crash, she left me and Dad with nothing but cows and a lot of heartache.

Angie and I drank our coffee in silence. Every time I looked up, she would force her eyebrows down. I played along, realizing how mad she really was. She knew my past, and she knew that I was going down the same road as my mom. Just like I hadn't deserved that, she didn't either.

I took a deep breath. "Ang, I know I've been a mess lately, and this is no excuse. I just have so many second thoughts about med school coming to an end. Dad's getting older, and I miss home. The city, the late nights, the *people* . . . It's really starting to get to me. I think I just need to clear my head. We have a short break before graduation, and I think I may need to go home again."

"And leave me in Denver? Alone?" She looked at me in disbelief.

Even though Angie was my best friend, she still didn't

know how much of my life was a lie. The drinking and the masking of emotions was starting to weigh on me. For so long it had been my way of pushing the past away. I was able to deflect my feelings, pretend I was social and happy with my achievements in life. I was burnt out. The more I pushed, the more the martinis, the Xanax, and the late nights at the bar weren't helping. I couldn't hide who I really was. I'd thought the fast-paced life was a salve that would heal my wounds, but it may have just been adding more salt.

The silence was her answer. That was the end of the conversation. She grabbed her yoga mat and headed out the door.

FOUR

As soon as I cleaned up one mess, another appeared.

> Are we still practicing for our interviews, or are
> you going to implode those plans too?

The text from Gabe had sat unread for the past two hours. Another friend I'd let down. I started typing, my fingers stumbling over the words to apologize. But I settled for a little less than the paragraph I deleted. Fourth year in medical school was all about residency and clinicals. The application process took up the first half of our fall semester, and we were entering the interview process. March was the month that the med school gods would decide our fate. I wasn't hopeful.

> Are you still at the park?

Almost immediately, my message was marked as read, and typing bubbles indicated that he had been waiting for my reply.

I never left my apartment. I figured you needed to sleep it off.

A sigh escaped me.

I'll meet you there in twenty minutes.

There was no time to shower, and I could still smell the vodka seeping out of my pores. I grabbed a cold wet rag from the shower and wiped my body from my neck down. Bottles of hairspray and medications tumbled out of the cabinet as I reached for the body spray. I pumped the fragrance all over myself, hoping to create the illusion that I wasn't actually an alcoholic.

My university sweatshirt and drawstring sweatpants passed the smell test, so I slipped them over my oily, stinking body. A toothbrush hung out of my mouth while I searched our apartment for the sample questions I'd written up.

The park was within walking distance, but I hopped in my Ford Ranger. I was already late and had received as much grace as I was going to get. When I turned the key, the truck let out a few whines before the engine revved, and I braced myself for the cold air the heater would blast at me. Traffic was light, and I took the same route I always did to get to our favorite spot. Angie had pointed out to me several times that there were shorter ways to get places, but this was what I knew, and there was no sense in changing it now.

It was afternoon, and the moms who brought their kids to the park to play were getting ready to head home for nap time. They packed up their strollers and wrangled angry three-year-olds who were fighting sleep. My gaze seemed to alarm them even though I was just waiting for a parking spot. I took a few laps around the park so they wouldn't feel anxious with me sitting there waiting. When a large white Suburban pulled out, I swerved into the open space.

The afternoon sun froze time. Before I could turn the key and grab my books, I sat in the warmth. Taking that moment to gather myself seemed appropriate after a morning spent lying to my best friend. I also had to hype myself up not to be an idiot around Gabe. I loved to hate him, and I hated to love him. No matter how many times I friend zoned him, he still treated me like the first day we'd met. He also still managed to make me uncomfortable in the most agonizing, thrilling way possible. He was obsessed with me, but I secretly felt the same way.

The park was almost empty. There were a few people walking their dogs, but as I watched through my front window, I couldn't help but scan the surrounding area for giant spaceships. Would I even see them, though? Did they all disguise themselves under the soil until it was their time to capture me?

They aren't going to abduct you in broad daylight in the middle of the city, you idiot.

Gabe sat facing away from me. I could see two coffees he'd picked up. He knew, and I knew, that he would take care of me. That night in the laundry room was the only time we'd both been drunk enough to act on the way we really felt for each other. The rest of our time in med school was spent seeing how many ways we could mask our feelings with crude humor and aggressive jokes. It was just as painful for me as it was for Angie to watch. In my heart, I felt a relationship would get in the way of my goals. I could hardly deal with my own feelings. How was I supposed to deal with somebody else's?

He'd asked if he could kiss me that night. The alcohol buzzed through my lips. My head felt like part of the air, floating around like a helium-filled balloon. The liquid courage lifted our spirits and broke down the barriers between us. It was the scary type of kiss—slow, meaningful, and controlled even though we were in a college rental's laundry room. The mismatched appliances were only props to hold myself up on. Because in my head, I was surrounded by blackness and intermittent colors that sparked each time our lips moved a different way. There was no dingy water smell, and I couldn't hear the music that blared in the next room. I remembered that night like it was yesterday. I'd never told him I thought of it every time I saw him. I wished I could do it all again.

My phone buzzed.

You OK?

The message from Gabe brought me out of my daze.

No, I thought. *I am in fact not OK.*

When I slammed the door shut, the metal creak and clank pulled him away from his phone and a smile stretched across his face. It disgusted me. How could someone know that a person was so unstable and continue to stick around? He shouldn't have been smiling. He should have at least tried to fake it like Angie. I wanted him to be mad at me. I deserved it.

"I'm surprised your shoes still fit this morning," he joked. My face must have been blank with confusion because he immediately added context. "From the martinis?"

"Oh, yeah. Sorry about the belligerent behavior. Rest assured, I was already disciplined by my other parent, Angie." I quickly added to the joke, hoping he didn't want to get into another deep conversation about my future.

"Jess, I'm not your mom." He reached a hand out to touch my arm.

"Yeah, I'm not either." I answered him by turning like I didn't see his gesture. He was used to it by now, but I don't think my resistance to his touch ever stopped hurting him. It also didn't help that the subject of my mom completely killed the mood. He knew my story a little too well. That's what happens when you get drunk on a regular basis and divulge all of your deepest emotions in one sitting.

Our arms brushed against each other, and I allowed it as we looked forward at the notes. There was a list of possible questions we'd come up with on our own. A breeze lifted the crunchy papers. I could tell he'd showered before he got here. The scent of aftershave and paper cleared my head a little from the hangover that still lingered. I took in a long huff, pretending I was stressed. What seemed like a frustrated sigh was really a chance to inhale more of his smell.

"It's alright, we have plenty of time. We can meet again tomorrow if you want?" He answered my stress with concern, another quality I didn't deserve. How long would he allow me to be close to him until he finally gave up? The guilt mingled with my anxiety, and I remembered I had a lot more to be worried about than my love affairs.

"What if I just didn't set up my residency?" I asked out of the blue. Light peeked through the trees, and the bare November branches made shadow pictures all over his face. It didn't matter what day it was, his hair was always perfectly trimmed and combed. I had never seen a single stalk of stubble poking from his face. His perfection and attention to detail was strange but attractive.

Gabe stared at me. "What do you mean, Jess?" He waited for an answer while I watched the light travel from one part of his face to another. The branches rustled much the way Scooby's legs had shifted in the grass back at the ranch. I was distracted, taking a warning from Mother Nature. I looked around once more before answering.

"What? Sorry. The last question you wrote down would really stump me. I think we should focus on that one," I lied.

"What would you do instead of medicine? It's all you've ever talked about since we met. You've already come this far . . ." His face resembled Angie's. Both of my friends were completely disappointed in my excuse. I'd been feeling this way since we started our last semester. The creeping thoughts of spying spaceships seemed to be a sign from God—or some space God? Who knows. It was the jolt I needed to take the thought of quitting seriously.

"What if we went abroad after March? We have a four-month break before we have to start residency. Maybe you just need a change in scenery?" Gabe had thought this through already. He wanted to go abroad. He wanted me all to himself. It would be his happily ever after. "You can't be serious," he added when I didn't answer. I'd joked about quitting a lot. I was comedic relief for most of our classmates, complaining about how hard things were even when I passed with flying colors.

I wanted to tell him that I couldn't mentally handle the stress, the hubbub of the city, *and* the secret I was keeping about almost being abducted by a large spaceship. But instead . . .

"I'm just kidding. You know I would never quit." I leaned my shoulder into him as I told my last lie.

"So traveling abroad isn't out of the question?" He squished his shoulder into mine, bringing his face a little too close to my hair. His lips and nose brushed against my greasy scalp, and when he didn't move away, I wondered if he was planning to fry an egg. Instead, he wrapped an arm around me and pulled me closer. A cool breeze whipped through the barren trees, and a slow, velvety shiver enveloped my body.

"Hmm. Maybe you're on to something." OK, one more lie.

That was not happening.

When I pulled away from his embrace, I took a final glance at our surroundings. The trees rustled once more, shaking as if in fear. The same feeling I'd had on the ranch crept down my neck, and my bones shivered in agreement. Intuition was something I tried not to believe in, but something told me this time, I needed to listen.

Whoever wanted me before, I had a feeling they were still watching.

CHAPTER
FIVE

By Monday morning, I had rid myself of all the alcohol in my system. The older I got, the harder it was to recover from my unhealthy coping mechanism. I'd applied to several orthopedic surgery residencies, and as my clinicals came to an end, I was taking on more and more responsibility. Today was judgment day.

Gabe waited for me outside. I caught myself triple checking my room for items that I didn't need. *Pat, pat, pat.* My hands searched my pocketless pants. Something seemed to be missing, but it wasn't a physical object I could hold. It was my brain. It seemed as though I was trying to pull it out of my ass so I wouldn't blow this clinical test.

"You ready for your big day?" Gabe shouted over his classic rock station when I got in the car. The air rushing in and out of my trachea produced a hollow sound, like wind whistling through an accordion straw. I climbed inside of the noise, trying not to let traffic, Gabe's voice, and his blaring music send me over the edge.

"Yep." My body stiffened, but when the car door shut, I found a little relief. Gabe looked forward. Today was a very important clinical, and it was pass or fail. When we finally arrived at the hospital, I let a breath escape with a low groan.

"Tell ya what, why don't we get through clinicals this week, and maybe Angie and I can plan some good old-fashioned fun this weekend? Movie marathon? Board games?" Gabe tried to stall my anxiety.

"I was actually thinking about going home this weekend. Dad's work has slowed down a little since he shipped out all his cattle. He's just taking care of pregnant cows now."

"Oh. Well, maybe that will be good for you. You've been really stressed lately. Can I at least come over Friday night? I'll bring takeout?" He raised his thick eyebrows. He wasn't giving up. I was stuck between a rock and a hard place. I could tell him no, which would only make him and Angie worry more. Or, I could say yes. That would satisfy them both, but I would have to keep lying to both of them.

"Alright. I want pizza and beer. And you're buying this time. I heard you guys charged your drinks to my card last weekend in retaliation for my behavior," I joked.

"It's a date." He loved saying that. I nodded as I stepped out of the car. The fall air was turning to a winter chill in Denver, and I prayed that snow wouldn't ruin my weekend plans. I just had to make it one more week before I could go and investigate more of the unknown. How long had these spaceships been around? What did they want from me? And why were they on the ranch?

I focused on my feet moving across the sidewalk, calculating the steps between each crack. Certain slabs of concrete were longer than the others, frustrating me when my numbers didn't turn out even. The cadence and the image of bright gray concrete reminded me of elementary school. With each step toward the hospital, I remembered the way I used to skip and run to the pickup line full of cars. I remembered searching for Mom's green Taurus. My flat Converse slammed against the hard ground, and it was almost like I could feel the shin splints that would inflict now.

I remembered throwing my bag into the car. Soot powder made its way through the vents and settled in the tan fabric seats. Mom's hair was thrown back in a knot that stuck out beneath an old ball cap. She had been helping Dad full-time on the ranch just before she died. Her job had fired her for calling off too much. It was the beginning of her end, but those few months where I got her full attention were the ones I held on to.

The daydream continued as I entered the hospital. Today's clinical hours had me assigned to a spinal surgery. Regret set in. I didn't want to do it anymore. I'd been so excited about it when I signed up over a month ago. Now I wanted nothing more than to go home and hide from the unknown. The elevator to orthopedics was empty, and my belly flipped when the jerky pully system transported me even further back into the memory.

Ten miles from town, twenty miles from home there was a landmark we knew as Galatea Road. There was an old run-down house, only the crumbling foundation left to commemorate the history of that time. It was our marker to turn home on dirt roads. Thirty miles was a long way for most kids to travel for school, but there was no traffic. All you saw were cornfields where the farmers worked, and pastures of grass where the cowboys took over.

Deer lingered in the ditches, and dusk painted the horizon with a camouflage fit for all animals. When Mom eventually had to flip on her headlights, the old green Taurus turned up clouds of dirt as we made our way home. Speckles of dust twirled in the light as we moved farther and farther into the cornfields.

Eight lights zoomed downward to face us, hovering.

The engine of the car hummed, softer, slower . . .

The elevator doors opened, and I scanned my student badge to get past the waiting room. My autopilot switched on as I made my way through the surgery wing. I found some scrubs to change into and a hairnet to cover my mop. I dressed slowly because there was more to the memory—something else had happened next. My mind just wouldn't get to the memory fast enough.

I'd noticed Mom had brought the car to a stop. Neither of us looked at each other. The lights had hypnotized us with fear and curiosity.

"Take a picture—hurry," she commanded.

Still entranced, I reached down for my hot pink Razr flip phone. And as soon as I flipped it open, the lights were gone. Did they turn off? Did whatever it was fly away?

No.

I shook my head as the memory faded, questioning whether I was in a different dimension—maybe parallel to the one I was living in before my accident at the ranch? Where had that memory come from? Had I shoved it away? We'd lost Mom in the car crash only a few weeks after that. It appeared my brain had been doing a great job of protecting me from something. But what?

The blue scrubs felt light against my skin as I made my way to the sink. I had been shadowing this doctor in particular for a few weeks now, and I had my preparation down. She waited as I ran soap over my forearms, scrubbing away anything that could make its way into the patient's system.

"Well, are you ready, Ms. Gray?" Dr. Graham's cap covered

her wild, curly blonde hair, and I focused on her hands as she washed them. She was inspiring, the way she worked so seamlessly through surgery. She saw potential in me; one more person I would eventually have to disappoint.

I pushed the memory away. Time to focus. "Yes, I've been looking forward to this! C3 and C4, right?" I'd been with her in the consultation when she explained how we would alleviate a herniated disc. We were performing a cervical discectomy and fusion. Dr. Graham would remove and replace the disc with a graft so the bones would eventually fuse together. I'd watched her complete several of these surgeries over the past few months, and now she was going to allow me to assist.

Dr. Graham's blade made an incision in the patient's throat. We'd planned for me to reach in with forceps to remove the damaged disc. The anesthesiologist gave me an encouraging smile as I moved to enter the slit in the skin. I found my way around her trachea, moving toward the back of her neck. An X-ray guided me between the two spinal vertebrae.

But before I could continue, the light above the surgery table seemed to flicker.

"You will remember nothing. Your mother died in a drunk driving accident. Her alcoholism led her to her grave." Dr. Graham seemed to be talking directly to me about my past, her eyes wide and hollow. But after a few blinks, I realized it wasn't her speaking.

She was saying my name. "Ms. Gray, I'm taking over." My hands were frozen over the incision.

I'd zoned out in the middle of surgery.

My brain was projectile vomiting more information that I had forgotten, and it had decided to do it right in the middle of a procedure I was supposed to perform. Everyone picked up my slack and completed the routine surgery while I watched from the sidelines in embarrassment.

I had failed.

But in that failure, there was another clue to my past. Another clue to who *they* were.

CHAPTER
SIX

Friday night arrived abruptly. I wasn't prepared to have both of my best friends in the same room. Between failing my clinical and the conjured memories, I was mentally losing at life. There was no energy left to fend off my worried friends.

It was two against one. They could play me back and forth until I caved. I wanted nothing more than to tell them, to share the burden with someone else. And for the first time since the incident, I wondered if I really was seeing things. Was I hallucinating? Was the pressure of school stirring up these feelings from my past? We'd learned about trauma and what it could do to the brain. Maybe the stress of my life was digging up these images, making me think that something was after me. Or was it the drinking and the pills catching up to me? I needed my friends. I wanted my friends.

Gabe busted down the door with his hip, a six-pack in one hand and a pizza box in the other. Angie frantically cleaned the living room as I sat at the bar of our apartment kitchen. Gray sweatpants hung low on Gabe's waist, and like usual his plain white T-shirt looked like it had been dry cleaned. I'd never seen a single wrinkle in his clothes. He was so put together even when we weren't supposed to be. It was nice to look at, but also unsettling.

I ran and slid across the tile floor straight to the sour beers he'd brought me, striking a dance move-style pose and cracking the top of one of the bottles while he opened the pizza box. Before I knew it, I was three beers in and throwing down pizza. For a minute, things seemed calm. The buzz of the alcohol started to turn off the noise, and I could actually hear what Gabe and Angie were talking about. Alcohol slowed down social interactions. It helped me focus on the conversation and not feel like people were perceiving me. I let my guard down a little bit and interjected myself in all the appropriate places.

The week had been particularly hard on everyone. We were all logging some serious clinical hours. Then there were the part-time jobs, not to mention feeding, drinking, and clothing ourselves. Our basic human needs were hardly being met because everyone else and medical school came first.

Angie broke down the pizza box to recycle and sprayed the counter down with cleaning solution. She never sat still; she physically couldn't. Instead of trying to stop her, Gabe and I had learned to stay out of her way.

"So, what are we going to watch?" I interrupted a story I had heard a million times—one about the time in undergrad when we took dead frogs and hid them in the women's bathroom in the library. Gabe and I watched as Angie whirled around the kitchen.

"I vote rom-com," Angie chimed in. Her eyes darted between me and Gabe, then back to me. She continued mopping the already clean floor.

"Horror flick, but like one of the old cheesy ones," Gabe said, diverting her.

"I vote horror! Sorry, Ang." I flashed a smile at Gabe and dropped my gaze when I scanned back to Angie. Her small figure bounced around the room as she looked for the remote, found the streaming app she wanted, and rearranged the blankets and pillows for us. Her enthusiasm exhausted me, but it was nice to feel a sense of comfort. Being with friends felt normal, or as normal as it could.

Just tell them.

Angie sat on one end of the couch, curled up as small as she could get. All I could see was her brown curls popping out of her hoodie. When I tried to sit close to her, she kicked me playfully, shoving me toward where Gabe would sit on the other end of the couch. My eyes rolled to the back of my head. When he sat, I quickly straightened and scooted my butt to the edge of the couch so neither of them could touch me.

And just as I popped the cap on my beer bottle, the title popped up on our screen: *Alien* (1979), Sci-fi Horror.

Jesus, Mary, Joseph, and all of the angels and saints. Of all the movies to pick.

Anxiety set in when I realized there was only one more beer on the counter. Maybe one more would give me the courage to come clean. If I had one more, maybe I would be able to just forget it altogether and move on with my life. It seemed like either way, I was losing.

Halfway through the beer in my hand, I felt tears welling up in my eyes. My nose started to fill with mucous, and I tried to disguise my fidgeting body as I began to cry. Only thirty minutes into the movie, I was bent over weeping. I couldn't escape the thoughts; they were infecting my reality.

"Jess? Hey . . . Are you . . . scared?" Gabe grabbed my shoulders. He knew I wasn't scared. But he could also tell that the cries I let out were fearful, though he had no idea why. Angie came out of her cocoon to pause the show. The light from the paused television shone onto concerned faces.

Tell them.

My heart seemed to be winning a battle over my brain. The alcohol distracted the giant organ in my head for the briefest moment, and I finally blurted it out.

"I've been having dreams. I think I've been hallucinating," I said.

"Are you reacting to the medications? The alcohol?" Angie lifted an eyebrow. She had warned me about this many lectures ago.

"What kind of dreams?" Gabe ignored Angie's comment.

"I've been seeing my mom everywhere. I keep having memories of when she was alive." My brain took over. Something in my subconscious told me that it wasn't safe to tell the truth—the whole truth. Both of them sat back, slightly relieved.

"They just feel so real, and a few of them make me think someone is watching me." I let my neck muscles relax so my head could fall into my hands in embarrassment. "I've been so freaked out lately, I just want to quit everything and go home."

That comment sent them both into full panic mode.

"It's completely normal to feel scared."

"Your life is stressful right now, and it's easy for your past to come up."

"You'll do great."

"We'll get you the help you need."

I couldn't even keep track of who was saying what. The noise in my head was back, and there was still no solution.

"I just need to go home and clear my head. I appreciate what you're trying to do, but I just can't do *this* anymore." I gestured around the apartment, reminding my friends that the city life, the constant pressure, and the socialization were breaking me. "I need some space, and I need you guys to trust that I will work this out." I stood up from the couch, staring at them with bloodshot eyes. They both nodded, knowing that fighting me would only make things worse.

I didn't need space. I needed to figure out what had happened in the pasture that day. I needed to figure out who had been watching me my entire life. What were those lights? And what had they done to Mom?

My feet failed me and I tripped, slamming my shin straight into the coffee table in the middle of the living room. The anger and frustration almost elevated my body, the rage carrying me into the bedroom. I slammed the door in their faces, slammed a Xanax down my gullet, and slammed my head into the pillow.

CHAPTER
SEVEN

MY FORD RANGER CREEPED OUT OF TRAFFIC, HEADING EAST ON I-70. The city turned to the suburbs. The large homes grouped together all looked the same, yet they were all slightly different, a repeating pattern of white, beige, black, and olive green. The distance wasn't much compared to the time it took to get that far out of town. Traffic clogged certain exits, and I hadn't anticipated the weekend congestion. Eventually I was out on the plains again. The number of traffic lights lessened as the distance between towns grew bigger. I stopped in Limon, a small town—not as big as Denver, but not near as small as my hometown.

I waited at the counter for my takeout order, tapping the surface anxiously. Each new location posed new threats, new places for things to hide. The loud cash register clanged as the employee calculated my order.

I knew Dad would be excited for a little treat. He didn't get out much, and it was an hour trek from the ranch to get some decent lo mein. I guess I should say *any* lo mein was at least an hour away.

Normal Jess would have been salivating waiting to dive into that Chinese, but my mind ached. It was in overdrive lately. I couldn't stop replaying the memories of my mom and the encounter with the spaceship. Plus, I kept rewinding the tape on every conversation that had happened over the past few weeks in Denver. I'd flagged Angie and Gabe's radar, but I didn't think they had a clue what was really going on. They knew Mom was a sore spot for me, and it was a great distraction to keep them from prying.

My stomach turned, reminding me that I was still a little hungover from the beer. Angie's coffee, Aleve, and toast combo was starting to wear off. She'd left it on my nightstand before I left, like she always did. Crying and storming off to my room had been a childish thing to do, but it was the perfect way to stall two people who acted as my second parents sometimes. They knew if I showed emotion, it must really mean I needed some space.

The highway sign read Kit Carson, 60 Miles. If I kept going, I could revisit my glory days of being a three-sport athlete, being involved in every extracurricular activity, and excelling in all of my classes. My mind flashed back to everyone's surprise when I was reading chapter books in kindergarten. I remembered my teacher not believing that I had already memorized all my states and capitals. The school achievements started very young, and I sometimes wished I had never presented my strengths. If I hadn't, maybe now I wouldn't be knee-deep in student debt and raging anxiety. I was burnt out. Instead of heading straight, I turned off onto dirt roads.

I turned my blaring music down, allowing myself to see better. The grass whispered back and forth, waving at me through my windshield.

Long time no see.

The familiarity of the landscape upset me. The kind sweet

nothings from the land were usually welcoming. Now they pestered me about the unknown beings that lurked about. I wondered if the calm rolling hills and patches of vegetation were as upset as I was. This space was supposed to be peaceful.

A few more turns got me home, but my lower back ached and my hands were clammy from the way I was gripping the steering wheel. My head was in protection mode, never allowing an inch of pasture to go unscanned the whole way home.

Dad waved to me from the front porch. I managed to wave back, my stomach dropping again. I contemplated asking him for a drink to get up the courage to tell him about what happened. My intestines twisted, urging me not to drink any more alcohol. I needed greasy food.

"Hey, Dad!" I shouted as I grabbed my bag from the bed of my little pickup. I dusted soot off, forgetting I had been on dirt roads for the last fifteen minutes.

"My favorite!" I heard the takeout bag crinkling. His smile reminded me of the simple things that made him happy. I was so used to eating out that I forgot what a treat it was when you lived in the middle of nowhere.

"I mean, it's nice to see you too." He chuckled as he threw an arm around me. This was a common interaction for us. I came home, we hung out, and then I brought myself back to reality and went back to school. But this time was different. This time, school wasn't the only issue.

Inside, I opened the plastic containers, condensation dripping onto the table.

"Sorry, Dad, you know it always gets kind of cold by the time I get here," I nervously interjected. I didn't need to do that, but I was on edge. The words came out shaky; a familiar amphibian seemed to be kicking the shit out of my uvula again.

Don't cry, Jess. Don't cry, don't cry, don't cry. Don't worry him.

"Jess, it's fine. That's what the microwave is for. I'm just thankful I don't have to cook myself dinner. I was literally going to eat a spoonful of peanut butter!" He smiled and sat down, waiting for a laugh even though he was being completely serious.

I managed a little smirk, glad that the food would provide some silence. It would also buy me some time to muster up the courage to start this conversation. I ate slowly, not pushing the limits with my sour stomach.

I stared across the room, focusing on the dark grain in the wood paneling of the old ranch home. The linoleum was clean, but the color was tinged yellow, permanently stained from the wear and tear of all the hired hands who'd lived here previously. Dad was a bachelor, but he wasn't a pig. The house had stayed as it was my entire life—old, tattered, but clean. A single glass, plate, and fork lay out on a dish towel, probably the only set he ever used after I left.

"Dad, have you ever seen anything weird out here?" I played with the lo mein noodles on my plate, not making eye contact.

He came up for air. For the past five minutes, I'd been afraid he would choke at the rate he was eating.

"Also, you should really start cooking more. You look thin," I added as he gathered himself. He wiped his silver mustache before continuing.

"What do you mean? Weird how? I see weird shit every day. And you live in Denver—I'm sure you see even weirder shit in the city, especially working in the hospital." He winked, taking a jab at the city folk. Dad was a vision of the Wild West frozen in time. He was proud of his roots. His sun-tattered skin was tough, his hands were mangled from accidents, and his eyes were soft. Because although his physical body had been through it all, his mind was clear. That was something a place like this was good for. It was the part that kept calling me back.

"I'm being serious, Dad. I just felt like there was a reason Scooby bucked me off last weekend. He's a spaz, but he's never bucked me off," I lied, remembering to keep my story straight. I wasn't ready to divulge the real reason I was hurt when he found me.

"You mean when you *fell* off?" he corrected me.

I answered his rude comment by lowering my eyebrows.

I stared at him for a few more seconds until he changed his demeanor. His blue eyes turned somber, and his bushy gray eyebrows furrowed. By the look of his wrinkles and the growing number of whites and grays, time hadn't stood still while I was gone away at school.

"Well, the plains of eastern Colorado hold more secrets than most of us would probably like to know. These lands were once inhabited by the Native Americans, and then the settlers from Europe came during the gold rush. I've seen things— maybe ghosts, supernatural things? I think that may be what you're asking?" he pried. I was trying to get it out of him without telling my side of the story. Then, if he said something crazy first, there wasn't much room left for him to judge me.

"Maybe I was in my head. Scooby just seemed off, and there wasn't an animal in sight for him to be freaked out by. I know he's skittish, and I know I'm prone to *falling* off." I rolled my eyes to lighten the mood. Maybe I could get something out of him if I played it off.

"You've always asked weird questions, just like your mom." Dad couldn't help but throw those little tidbits in as often as he could. I was the only way to keep his memory of Mom alive. We talked of her often, but even after all these years, it didn't make it hurt less.

He sat slumped over from all the food as I started to clean

up. I could tell he was pondering the question, searching for what he wanted to tell me.

"You know, there was one time in particular." He paused, looking around at the ceiling, recreating the picture in his head.

"When your mom first passed, I guess I kind of thought I was . . . Well, you know . . . losing it? I had this odd feeling that someone was watching me. You know how quiet it gets down here." He pulled his Copenhagen Long Cut out of his front shirt pocket. He packed it over and over, forming a C with his fingers around the round container.

Thunk. Thunk, thunk, thunk. I watched him impatiently, trying not to show how anxious I was to hear the rest of the story. I did know how quiet it could get out here. There was a reason I came back every time I was about to have a mental breakdown. But at the same time, when you were alone and you really paid attention, it could be unsettling. The only sounds were the regular rhythms of the ranch. You could hear the gates squeaking to open, squeaking to close. The grain pouring into the horses' pails. Cows bellowing, the old work trucks rumbling.

But sitting there after all the work was done—that, my friends, was something only a few of us could understand.

He took a pinch of tobacco and packed it in the lower right corner of his mouth, nice and tight. I watched the bulge begin to calm him, realizing he'd put a dip of nicotine in to prepare himself for the rest of the story.

"So I was in the shop, working on one of our pickups. You were at your friend's house in town. You remember Katie? Their parents offered to give me some time to myself after the funeral, and you needed a distraction . . . It was summertime, and the sun was just starting to go down. I obviously had drunk quite a few buckskins by then. That's partly why I've never told anyone this story, because maybe I was shit-faced?" He smiled, the bulge of tobacco stretching his bottom lip.

"Dad, get to the story," I coaxed, adding a smile to encourage him to go on. My face was calm, but I tapped my foot on the floor. I pressed my thumb against all four of my other fingers, repeating the sequence over and over, trying to calm myself. *One, two, three, four . . . One, two, three, four . . .*

"Well, anyhow, I cleaned up and decided I would just walk home. It was about eight o'clock, right when dusk hit. I could see well enough to make it two hundred yards to the house. But even after I left the shop, I still had a strange feeling like someone was watching me. And I can't describe it, Jess, but I really wasn't scared. It always felt like maybe your mom was trying to tell me something. Right as I passed the cattle guard, the horses started running like crazy out of the corrals. They were hootin' and hollerin', kicking and carrying on. I ignored that too. But then, the entire sky lit up." He stared at the ceiling, transported by the memory.

"Was it a thunderstorm, like lightning?" I was trying to debunk my own theories, but I couldn't get the weird lights out of my head either.

"No, not a cloud in sight all day. But I swear to you, Jess, it felt like the entire world was lit up, like the middle of the day. But there was no sun. I was so taken back I just sat there, staring like a deer in headlights—"

"And then what?" I lost it. I needed more information, and this story was only confirming that I wasn't crazy—that there was shit happening I couldn't explain either. Which was worse, seeing this stuff for real, or being sent to the looney bin?

"It went dark." He hit the table and turned to open the fridge. Coors Banquet bottles lined the bottom shelf. He didn't have food, but there was always beer and tobacco on hand.

"Never really believed in God, but instead of blaming the

alcohol, I believed it was either Him or your mom telling me that it was going to be OK." He turned from me while he opened his beer, the top popping off into the trash. I knew that was all I was going to get from him.

I didn't pry, because I could tell the frog was in his throat now, and neither of us could handle him crying.

CHAPTER
EIGHT

I THREW MY HAND OUT TOWARD MY NIGHTSTAND, FORGETTING I wasn't in Denver. I swatted around, looking for my phone to reorient myself.

Four a.m.

I didn't know whether I should try to go back to sleep or just stay up. Dad would be up in an hour, and I'm sure he'd want my help with the morning chores. I sat up, taking both of my hands and rubbing at the knots that had taken residence in my face muscles. This was what it was like every single morning. The booze, the painkillers, the anxiety meds—none of it made my mind turn off. Ever since the accident, I hadn't been able to function.

Every time I went through a stressful situation, it was harder and harder for me to regulate. I turned to the substances because I didn't know how else to cope. It took all of me to fit in, to seem like I was *normal.* This tension added to my social anxiety, my overwhelm, and the mask that I wore all day. I had to remember to smile and make eye contact. I had to be sure that there was someone present in my eyes, trying to keep from losing myself in my own thoughts. This new addition to my mental load was getting hard for me to carry. At the moment, all that weight seemed to be held inside my jaw. I opened my mouth, stretching the muscles as much as I could before I got up.

I heard rustling in the kitchen. From the sounds of it, I wasn't the only one who couldn't sleep.

Dad and I had learned to cohabitate with little to no talking. It was never uncomfortable for me; it wasn't for him either. Mom was always the talker, and I guess that was one thing that I didn't get from her. Instead I took on Dad's more reserved characteristics. It definitely added to my struggles at school. Because although I could excel in academics, the socializing took every ounce of my being. The older I got, the more I realized why Dad wanted to work out here. The work was hard, but the interaction with people was very minimal.

Bacon sizzled in the pan, and Dad already had pancakes buttered and ready to eat. I hated breakfast, but I knew I'd better eat now or I would be dying by noon when he was still finishing up work. In the transition from fall to winter, the ranch was always fairly slow, but Dad operated based on what needed done, not a nine-to-five schedule. Half of his workload had been shipped off to feed the people of the United States. The other half was in the form of baby calves growing in the bellies of all the mama cows that still inhabited the ranch.

We moved in silence, grunting, clearing our throats, and cleaning the kitchen after we ate. I found my warm clothes where I'd left them last. There was still mud on my hoodie from where I fell, taunting me. Each time I got too comfortable, the little voice in the back of my mind made sure I knew why I was really home. The mudroom had made my clothes cold to the touch, matching the day that awaited us on the other side of the front door. Just like Dad had that feeling that someone was watching him, I continued to wonder if the lights were real and why they were coming around more frequently.

Who controlled the lights? Who wanted to see what we were up to?

Dad had already started the maroon Chevy, its diesel engine purring in front of the house. The exhaust roared as it idled, and I watched steam cloud the air.

"Ready Freddy?!" Dad shouted, startling me out of my thoughts.

"Let me grab my coffee!" I darted for the kitchen. Dad waited for me to realize he'd already prepared my coffee tumbler for the road. He held it in the air as I closed the front door and he dipped into the pickup. The best part about coming home during fall and winter work was the warm heater and the road coffee.

As we drove from tank to tank breaking the cattle's ice, it almost seemed like nothing ever happened. I contemplated pretending that the spaceship situation didn't exist. It had stolen the solace of home from me. It took the one place I considered a refuge and threw it in my face. I was forced to be haunted by my conscience until I found out what happened.

An icy gust whipped around us, the uneven air pressure screaming across the frozen dirt clods. I watched for the soft conversation of the grasses, the sagebrush, and the yucca. They were muted by the cool wind. I looked to where the hills met the sky and still could not see a spaceship.

I leaned on my pitchfork while Dad swung his axe into the layer of ice protecting the water from the cows' slobbery noses. I guess I should have done the heavy lifting since I was younger and more agile, but our father/daughter relationship hadn't changed since I was little. He broke the ice, I fished out the pieces.

The cows waited patiently. Frost covered their black hair,

and they let out their breath like a smoker who'd just taken a long drag. Fog released instead of smoke, but the image of a nicotine-addicted cow made me laugh. The physical activity kept me warm, but each time I stopped moving, the cold took tiny bites out of my skin.

Crack! A big slab of ice broke into two pieces. The liquid sloshed, rocking the small icebergs around as Dad continued to crush them into smaller chunks for me. Really, my job wasn't that hard; I was more there for the company, but I fiddled, so it took me way longer than it should have. I looked up, scanning the horizon, looking for answers. All I found was gray and brown pastures, frozen solid. We had come over a hill to get to this tank and it made me aware of how alone we really were. This was how alone Dad was every day of his life. It was beautiful, but the quiet that you could almost feel creeped down the back of my neck.

I fished out the last piece of ice, ready to get back to the warm vehicle.

I turned—

With an impact that was almost like an embrace, arms wrapped around where my elbows bent.

I tried to scream, but a black cloth bag was swiped over my face, my inhale pulling the fabric into my mouth.

I heard hooves scatter, and I listened hard.

The old Chevy still hummed in the background.

"Daaaaaad!" In my mind I screamed, but all that came out was a muffled garble.

CHAPTER
NINE

FLUORESCENT LIGHTS GLEAMED DOWN ON ME. I LOOKED AROUND, trying to get my bearings, but I felt more hungover than after a night of filthy martinis. The small box I was contained in resembled an interrogation room, and I looked for a two-way mirror like in the movies. There weren't any windows or mirrors, but there were two cameras in the corners of the room in front of me. I was sitting on an old pleather couch. I picked at the pieces that were peeling off as I continued to assess the vague place where I now found myself.

On the left side of the room was a metal door, and the walls were rebar and concrete. I was most likely in some type of basement. I wasn't chained up or anything, though, so why the dramatics? I rolled my neck every ten seconds or so. I noticed I was also pressing my fingers to my thumbs again.

One, two, three, four . . . One, two, three, four . . .

When I missed my pinky, I started counting backward, starting a new rhythm. I paused, taking my two index fingers and pressing down on my thumbnails, finding comfort in the pressure. The last time I'd done two of my fidgets at once was in elementary school when I got yelled at by the teacher for distracting the class. My nerves were bringing out a side of me that I could no longer push away.

Focus, Jess. Do aliens have basements with rebar and concrete? I'm still on this Earth, right?

Obviously, I wasn't stupid enough to try to escape a room with cameras. Where was I going to go? There was probably someone waiting right outside for me with their weird sedative drugs.

Do aliens have shit like that too?

The door jiggled. I crammed my entire body into the corner of the old couch, barricading myself as if the tattered material would shield me from whatever was about to come.

"Jess . . ." A familiar voice squeaked behind the door. As it slowly creaked open, I leaned out of my crouched position. Whoever it was wasn't moving fast enough to satisfy the curiosity that was building in the pit of my stomach. Aliens or not, I needed to know what the hell was happening already.

"So, let me exp—"

"GABE?!" I shouted in disbelief. Before I knew it, I was off the couch, toe to toe with one of my best friends.

"What the actual fuck?!" I was at his throat now, my words cutting the air between us like staccato daggers. Each one sliced a part of his face, keeping him from answering my questions.

When I ran out of curse words and air to breathe, I finally noticed that he had grabbed my arms. My fists were clenched, ready to hit him, and the only thing stopping me was his familiarity.

"Jess, can I talk?" Gabe looked at me with his massive green eyes. If I hadn't just been kidnapped in the middle of a pasture, I would think he looked slightly pitiful.

Before I could answer him, he blurted out, "I'm in the CIA." He knew that was the only way that I would listen, because nothing else about this was making sense. "I'm on special assignment—Project SPECTRUM."

I stared at him. My eyes glossed over as I replayed every memory I had of him since we'd started school eight years ago. He was just a little dweeb. Yeah, he had that sandy hair, and those eyes. They rounded as I studied the backlog in my brain. He looked at me the same way he did every time I drank, every time I did something questionable. The math was not mathing. He watched the corner of my mouth turn downward and the eleven between my eyebrows crease.

"I'm a little older than I said. They assigned me this position because of how young I looked. Look, I know this is a lot to take in, and I know I was on assignment, but that doesn't mean this was all a lie." He rushed his words and held his hands out in front of him, palms facing down. It was his silent plea for me to simmer down before he had to call in the bigwigs who actually looked like CIA agents. *Aren't they all old and chiseled and wearing sunglasses?*

My brain buzzed. I could hardly focus on everything that was happening. I was still processing that someone I'd made out with in a laundry room when I was twenty-two was the same person who'd kidnapped me. He shut his mouth when he saw my eyes come back into focus. The last thought I had was of Will Smith and Tommy Lee Jones walking through Denver with big space guns killing aliens. That was when I realized I had spiraled too far.

"So you aren't a doctor?" I waited for him to respond, but he didn't speak. "Since none of it was a lie, I'll treat you just like I always have. You're a coward. Are you going to tell me what's going on now? I don't have time to process. I thought I was seeing things. I thought I was crazy, and now I don't know what to think!" I talked through my teeth, my mouth never completely opening.

"That's why I'm here! And, no, I'm not a doctor." He continued to hover his arms in the air, trying to settle me. All it did was annoy me even more.

"So I work in a division that works with . . . extraterrestrial beings . . ." He waited for me to chew his ass out again.

"Yeah, and? They've been extra extraterrestrial lately, in case you haven't noticed!" I couldn't get my jaw to open. My teeth were about to break with anxiety and anger.

"Long story short, we've had eyes on you since you were little. For some reason, they have a high interest in you, your family, and possibly the location of the ranch that you grew up on. There've been multiple sightings of lights that can't be explained. They're never detected in our airspace. We aren't really sure all of the details. All we know is that . . ." He trailed off, looking down at his feet.

I blinked in anger, raising my eyebrows, signaling for him to continue.

He looked up from his slick suede shoes. My eyes locked with his, and I disappeared again into my head. News headlines, vodka bottles, and the mangled sight of the little Ford Taurus Mom used to drive back and forth from town flipped through my head. The images repeated over and over.

"Jess . . . ?" Gabe's voice pulled me from the depths of the highlight reel, and as my eyes focused, I realized I had been staring into his soul. I sat on the edge of the couch with my legs crossed. My foot bounced.

One, two, three, four . . . One, two, three, four . . . I concentrated on the rhythm of my fingers hitting my thumb. I had to get control of my nerves before I could answer him.

"One more thing." Gabe's lips disappeared into a thin line

where his mouth should have been. He lifted his brows, squinting his eyes.

"Jesus Christ," I blurted out and sighed. I put my face in my hands, not prepared to hear any more.

"We believe that whatever it was killed your mom."

CHAPTER

TEN

IT TURNED OUT I WASN'T TOO FAR OFF WITH MY *MEN IN BLACK* RABBIT hole. Gabe told me that Mom was an agent. She'd decided to move on from the CIA and agreed to let them completely wipe our memories so we could start all over. She wanted to enjoy her new family and live out her days on the ranch in peace. But for some reason, I still remembered a lot. My memory had been wiped several times over because I had been telling people about odd things that happened to me. I was going to school and telling them I saw aliens. I was saying I saw odd lights, and I knew information that I shouldn't. For some reason, their technology hadn't worked on me. The agents had a device that used hypnosis technology. It wrapped around your head, forcing you to look into the swirling images. All the while they had earpieces feeding you the specific information they wanted you to forget. They did this to me, and they did this to Dad. Except with Dad, it worked.

Gabe handed me a file, revealing a badge photo of Mom. Her warm smile was gone, her mouth pulled into a thin line. Even in the picture, you could tell she was hiding something.

The file also contained fake news reports about the car crash and a fake death certificate.

Lies upon lies upon lies.

Gabe watched me as I took in the information. He was reciting lines like he'd practiced them for weeks. There was a sense of fear in his tone, and I got the feeling he was trying to earn his keep here. He tripped over his words several times, forgetting where he was in his prepared speech. I felt like I was at a high school public speaking event. It was painful and frustrating. I had an image in my mind that people who worked for the government were elite. I'd never pictured the rambling mess in front of me.

"So you knew something happened a few weeks ago?" I interrupted his monologue, catching him in a pause that he wasn't ready for.

"Yeah," he answered shortly and continued on about how the CIA was there to protect us, and blah blah blah.

"So, you're telling me that you have no idea what these weirdos want? What do they want with me? I'm one blackout away from getting thrown in the drunk tank," I snapped. The story was making sense, but it wasn't the full truth. Something was missing, and oddly enough, I thought Gabe believed it. But I didn't.

"We don't know, and with the increased sightings around the ranch and the memory wiping not working on you, we decided to try and use this as an opportunity to figure out what exactly they want." His demeanor was all business, but I saw glimpses of the person I knew peeking through. He was pleading with me to take whatever bait they'd told him to offer me.

"Your mom knew something, and she moved you in order to keep you safe," he added.

"Alright, well I'm going to pretend to believe you, but first you need to tell me what your real name is and where my dad is." I raised my eyebrows, treating him the way I always had. Title or not, I wasn't scared of him.

"Nathan Gabriel Harris." He rolled his eyes.

"So the name wasn't a total lie?" I prodded.

"Your dad is next door." Gabe picked up his papers and left the room, seeming unsatisfied. That made two of us.

I was able to meet Dad in the next room. They'd grabbed him on his way back to the pickup. His room was similar, except his had a cloth couch, which freaked me out. I always thought of all the dead skin cells that sloughed off onto furniture and mattresses.

"I asked when we could go home. At least we got the last tank broke. I fed the dogs when we left too." Dad tried to lighten the mood with his word diarrhea. It made me more uncomfortable than the silence. We both stared at the rebar across from us, contemplating our entire lives, wondering which parts were real, who was undercover, and who we could believe. Why did I remember so much more now? How had these memories been unlocked?

"Honestly, Dad, I admire your dedication to the animals, but that's the least of my worries. We just found out we've been watched my entire life by a group of aliens who most likely killed Mom. I couldn't care less if the 500 head of Black Angus die. The dogs—well, they'll get creative," I answered with a blank stare, still looking forward. A tinge of guilt washed over me. I noticed he hadn't taken his eyes off of me since they put us in the same room. He didn't answer, and I knew I'd hurt his feelings. He'd been clueless up until now. For me, the explanation felt like a relief. But my poor dad was in shock.

"They claim they don't know why they only watch us. They

occupy our land, keep tabs on us. They act like this is all a mystery, but let's be honest, Dad. There's more to the story." I finally met his gaze, noticing the fear in his eyes, the desperation for normalcy. We were no strangers to conspiracy theories, but the only problem was, this wasn't a theory. The extraterrestrials were real, and we were their targets.

We were both sworn to secrecy in exchange for heightened protection. There would be agents in and out of our lives, and we were instructed to "lay low" and "act normal." They were planning to use us as leverage to gain information. I wasn't sure what they wanted, but they sure didn't want me digging around to figure out what it was. Gabe had seen me freak out the other night. That was why they finally had to let us in on the secret.

We waited with Styrofoam cups and shitty drip coffee. The least they could have done was bring our to-go tumblers. I craved my piping hot percolated brew.

"I always wanted to move away from the city, Jess. Your mom told me when you were born that we needed to save our money to get our little place. I just assumed she wanted to raise you in a smaller town, live off the land. She was always wary of the city; she didn't trust very many people. Since I grew up out on the eastern plains, I knew the cattle business from the day work jobs I started when I was thirteen. It was our new start in life—a great way to raise you. I never could have expected this." His eyes drooped as he spoke. He was questioning Mom's intentions, and so was I.

What did she know that we didn't?

Rather than responding, I put my arms around him. We silently agreed to stop talking, knowing that there was too much to process. These people were supposed to keep us safe, but deep down I think we both knew that only we could keep each other safe. I wasn't really a match for the CIA and US government entities, so I decided to go along with the charade until I could find out more.

As we chewed on our thoughts, Gabe walked in with some other agents. They didn't seem as friendly, and there was less chitchat. Dad asked them who would be watching the ranch, but they answered with unimpressed stares. Gabe looked at me with sadness, and I realized he wasn't allowed to divulge any more. The only nugget of truth he could give was that he was undercover, and he was helping protect us from unfamiliar life-forms. He'd said they drove vehicles with eight lights in a predictable pattern. There were four on the main cabin, and two on each wing. Once the memory conjured itself up from my childhood, I matched it with the aircraft I'd fallen from. It wasn't much information, but it was a start.

They directed us to a hallway also lit with fluorescent lighting. It was so bright you couldn't see very far in front of you. The hallway was lined with two other weird rooms. I wondered how many old used couches they had in there. You'd think the CIA could invest in better furniture.

I knew it wasn't the right time, but I studied Gabe from behind. I just couldn't fathom that he was some kind of undercover CIA badass. How was *he* going to save *me*? It was hard for me to get past seeing him as my best friend. He was obsessed with me—very openly obsessed with me. But maybe he had to pretend he was obsessed with me? Being bamboozled was really starting to piss me off.

His white shirt was tight over his broad shoulders. His rolled sleeves strained against the crease where his biceps ended. My eyes shifted down to his belt as he continued to walk down the hallway.

Jesus Christ, Jess.

I caught myself before I could examine him any further. Maybe he was hot, I don't know. I was big into personality, and I guess his meek, puppy-dog attitude for the last eight years had been a real big turnoff. Regardless, I checked him out in anger, realizing that not only was his personality a lie, but he had been hiding this strangely attractive side the entire time. I always thought he was attractive, but this? This was different. When he was with me, he was so meek, so loving. The minute the other agents came around he flipped the script. He stood a little taller, spoke with a frank ease I wasn't used to. Which part was real?

And now I was supposed to just pretend everything was the same and he wasn't the person hiding the real reason behind Mom's death.

"Jess, we get to go home. Let's just focus on the good," Dad said in answer to my confused look. He looked at me out of the corner of his eye while we made our way out into a parking garage. An older man and woman in black suits waited by the door.

"Agent Harris will escort you home. He will be your point of contact until we can get these sightings under wraps. If you need anything, feel free to contact him. If we find out that you've told anyone about what's happening, you will be held here indefinitely." The woman looked at me, looked at Dad, and then turned around. The large bald man followed her inside and we were left with the new and improved version of Gabe.

"So, do I still call you Gabe? Let's pretend you're still the lame little med student who's in love with me." I winked with sarcasm. I was trying to be funny, maybe make a joke, but like I said, that part of "Gabe" was gone. I was dealing with Nathan now. Or should I say, Agent Harris.

"I'm still a friend, Jess. I just have a gun and a title now, that's all." He winked back. Our world thus far had been situational. He was a boy who'd been getting in the way of my goals. But now he was a man trying to protect me. The same person had completely morphed in a matter of twenty-four hours.

He led us into a black sedan. The windows in the back were tinted so we couldn't see out. I studied Agent Harris, feeling frustrated, angry, and curious. I had seen these types of situations in the movies many times, but I couldn't get over how defeated I felt.

Human interactions were already hard for me, and now I was going to have to pretend to know Gabe in front of everyone who didn't know him as Nathan. I'd lost my mask. I feared that I wouldn't be able to hold in what was really happening, especially around Angie. After the hissy fit I'd thrown the other night, I was sure Gabe was worried too. I was like a soda you shake up and hand over without the person knowing. Once Angie popped the tab, it was going to spew a mess all over the place.

Dad sat next to me making small talk. He drank his nasty coffee, acting like it wasn't the worst thing he'd ever tasted. Dad had a way about him where he could just act oblivious to the world around him, ignoring the fact that we were in danger and that everything we knew was a lie. When we neared the exit of the parking garage, light shone through the car. I went to peek my nose between the two front seats to try and gauge where we were. Before I could get a peek, Gabe was rolling up a black divider, shielding us from the outside world.

Luckily, we were in Colorado, and the weather was so unpredictable that the water didn't freeze as hard as it had before we were kidnapped. We had been in holding for twenty-four hours. It wasn't enough time for the animals to die off, but it was enough time to fall behind.

A weekend meant to calm my nerves turned out to be more like shock therapy. But there was one small sliver of clarity as I anticipated how my life would change moving forward.

Mom didn't leave us.

She was trying to save us.

CHAPTER

ELEVEN

"So, I'll see you in class?" Gabe winked at me as I stepped out of the vehicle. Dad put out his hand for a handshake. My hand involuntarily went to my forehead. I wasn't sure if he was asserting his dominance or keeping up the charade that he was cool with everything that had just happened.

"Yeah, I guess I'll see you next week." I slapped a smile on my face. He nodded as he got back into his car. As he drove away, the dirt billowed behind him. When he cleared the hill out of our circle driveway, Dad and I both found our way back inside the house.

He shuffled around the mudroom and pulled out an old cooler. Rummaging through the spare fridge that he kept medicine in for the cattle, he pulled out two ice packs and threw them at the bottom. Without a word he walked to the fridge and started packing Coors Banquets. The glass clanged together and I realized it really was a charade. He was a mess, and the next thing I saw was his Copenhagen being ripped out of his front pocket.

"Let's go feed," he murmured, and I saw tobacco sprinkle his shirt as he put in a dip.

And he's back.

I followed him out the door, grabbing some koozies from the junk drawer to the right of the kitchen sink. I didn't want my hands getting cold. I kept my mouth shut as he loaded the cake feeder. He backed up aggressively, a little too fast. The Chevy had magically made it back to the house after they took us. That was another issue—why couldn't they have just asked us to come with them? Then I looked at our current situation. There was a rifle Dad kept behind the seat for coyotes, a cooler full of beer, and axes and shovels strapped behind the cake feeder.

Yeah, OK. There was no way we were going to go willingly.

The pickup jerked me forward when Dad slammed on the brakes. He pulled the lever to fill the boxy feeder with pellets. The large pieces of food resembled a rockslide as gravity let them down the funnel.

As we waited, Dad cracked open a beer and handed it to me. He opened his and motioned with his finger for one of my koozies. We drove down the county roads, finding our way to the cattle. Two-tracks led us to groups of cows that were clearly annoyed. They knew we were late, and they swarmed the pickup before we could even gather a count.

I kept my mouth shut as I continued drinking my beer. Dad was already on his second, and I didn't question him. We repeated this in several pastures, making sure all the cows were fed. I waited patiently for him to get enough booze in him to figure out how he wanted to talk about what had just happened. I wasn't the only one who was terrible at facing their problems.

"You really think they don't know why these 'aliens' are after us? They really think we're some dumb, gullible country bumpkins?" Brown saliva shot all over the steering wheel along with his words. He took one of his empty bottles and spit his wad of chew in it. I waited for him to roll his tongue around, cleaning all the tobacco from his lip, teeth, and cheeks. He looked down at me over his nose, still aiming leftover tobacco into the brown bottle.

"Can we also talk about the fact that Mom was *murdered?*" I emphasized my anger in all of the r's in "murder." He was finally speaking my language, and I was happy to share my outrage with the only other person who'd just experienced what I had.

Although the current situation was unnerving, it was comforting that I wasn't keeping secrets anymore. I could finally speak freely about all the things that had been happening to me. Everything was out on the table with the only person I felt I could trust. Well, other than Angie. Dad and I both divulged all the weird things that had happened on the ranch that we'd discredited. I told him about the time Mom and I were driving home. I told him the truth about my accident with Scooby. He watched me tell my stories without judgment, because he had seen even more than I ever had. Like he'd said before, he always chalked it up to his depression, his sadness at Mom's passing, and the drinking.

"Kid, I just wish I knew what happened before she died. It's like a black hole every time I look back to see her. There's nothing left of her in my memory, other than you and how much I loved her. She's gone." Dad seemed to dig through the creases of his brain, searching for the real image of her. "I'm jealous you remember her taking you to school, because everything they erased is gone forever."

"I don't think she was an alcoholic, Dad. That was their story, but we have to figure out what really happened before they wiped us. Whatever got her could be after us too," I added. The pickup bounced over a few bumps and beer fizzed over our hands.

The cattle were fed, and the beer was gone. When we came back inside, I started washing potatoes to get some food in our stomachs before we took the drinking a little too far. The stove clicked as Dad lit the flame to heat the cast iron full of oil. I left the skins on, chopping home fries and looking for some hamburger in the fridge. I settled for a single tube of breakfast sausage.

With two pans going, I took out a package of tortillas along with some shredded cheese. Nothing could fix a sad, confused, angry person like some meat and potatoes in a sloshing stomach full of beer. I was relieved to see Dad go to the water-cooler instead of to the fridge for more alcohol. He drank a few sips as he set the table.

Like usual, we grunted around the kitchen, remembering the rhythm of life we'd learned without Mom years ago. The sausage and potatoes fried together, and the heat melted the cheese I sprinkled over the top. I threw tortillas on the hot cast iron, flipping them quickly with my bare hands, trying not to burn myself.

When we sat down to eat, we both realized how hungry we were. They'd offered us food at the creepy underground CIA mystery basement, but neither of us could eat. I think we also realized we were both a little buzzed and needed to ground ourselves before we moved forward with the events of the week.

"Mom knew something," Dad said between bites of crunchy potato. He continued eating, and we both mulled over the possibility that they killed her because of what she knew. But why would they keep coming back for us? I didn't know how all of this worked, but if they were smart enough to fly their fancy spaceships here, wouldn't they already know that we couldn't remember anything?

"There was a reason we moved out here, and she knew something was coming for us," he continued as he found his favorite grain on the wood-paneled wall in front of him.

"Yeah, except it's still coming for us," I replied with a mouth full of food.

"I think the government needs something from us too." Dad scooped the remaining hash into his tortilla.

"So what's our plan now?" I asked.

"I think we need backup." He rubbed his full stomach.

But who?

CHAPTER

TWELVE

I PACKED MY BAGS MONDAY MORNING AND FOUND MYSELF TRAVELING back into the concrete jungle. Dad had plans to vaguely discuss "trespassing" with the neighbors. We both thought it was a great way to have others keep an eye out for invaders without having to tell them the whole truth. The rural community was tight-knit and looked out for one another. If we disappeared, at least someone would know.

The plains were barren, and I pictured what the aliens looked like. Were they green like the little toys I used to get from the quarter machine? Did they have multiple arms, legs, eyes? Did they breathe oxygen? Were they smarter than us? I wondered if they were hiding, waiting for Dad to go feed cattle, lurking under the sagebrush again. Gabe assured us that there would be 24/7 surveillance in the sky above the ranch head-quarters. We would be the first to know if there was any activity. But for some reason, I didn't think I could trust that little weasel. After all, he had been lying for the past eight years of undergrad and med school. What else was he hiding?

Angie looked refreshed when I walked into our apartment.

The tension had dissipated. It was a relief too, because I couldn't handle her being mad at me. It didn't fit her kind nature, and it was painful to watch.

"How was home? The fresh smell of cowshit clear everything up?" She giggled, really impressed by her joke. Angie was everything that I was not. She was charming in a bubbly, girly type of way. She was probably the only reason I had any friends, because otherwise I would just sit in my room and binge-watch murder documentaries by myself. Comfort shows were more enticing than what the real world had to offer.

"You could say that," I lied, but it was also the truth. I really did clear some *shit* up. It didn't exactly solve any problems, but at least I could rule out the looney bin. "Hey, Ang?" I asked for her full attention. "I'm really sorry for what I've put you through with the drinking, the anxiety, and anything else I've done to stress you out. I know you care about me, and I need to start doing the same for you."

She made me sit on that one. I lifted my left eyebrow, raising the entire side of my face. She watched me squirm in my guilt for a little while before answering.

"I *know* you love me, and I know I worry too much sometimes, but I'm having issues too. What happens now? I still don't know which residency program I want to go to. I didn't apply to very many places either. I'm so tired, Jess, so tired. I guess I just got fed up with it always being about you." She looked down and I knew she had been reciting that in her head the entire time I was gone. I wasn't mad either. She was right. I took advantage of Angie's loving nature all the time. It wasn't fair that she became the mother figure in my life at the age of eighteen.

From the day she sat next to me in our first biology lab, she had been taking care of me. I'd left my dissection kit in my dorm room, and she was there with an extra. That single scalpel knife was the beginning of our friendship. We bonded over our parental abandonment issues and our hopes of being part of something much larger than ourselves. She coped much better than I did with the stress of our lives, and she suffered because of it. She was emotionally supporting me when she should have been enjoying her college years. For that, I was forever grateful.

It was hard for her to tell me that she wanted to come first for once. Her hair was disheveled, and she hadn't moved from the couch since I left. Takeout boxes were scattered all over her room. We were both really going through it, and I had been so blinded, and I couldn't explain to her why.

"You're completely valid, Ang. I've been a total asshole, and I can't do life without you either. Let's both figure our shit out and move forward with our lives. We can be adults and still be scared." I hugged her tiny body, forcing out a groan. She always joked that I was so tall because, where I come from, we're cornfed. My five-foot-ten athletic build always dwarfed her. It was a running joke that maybe the only reason she kept me around was for protection.

"Speaking of adulting, our lease is up in March. We should know where we got assigned for residency by then. You give any thought to whether you're going to stick around Denver?" She scrunched her eyes with a smile, clearly hoping my softened state would help me decide to stay.

"I said we would figure our shit out, but I didn't mean all in one day." I released her from my aggressive hug. "How about we have some fun this week and get ready for the end of this semester? I don't want to think of any adulting until then!" I held on to her shoulders, coaxing the scrunchy smile to return to her face.

"You're right. Where should we start?" She looked around the room. I followed her gaze and realized maybe we should clean. There was no way she would have any fun if the apartment was covered in fermenting cherry limeades and crusty Styrofoam boxes.

We spent Thanksgiving together in our apartment, and the first week of December livened up the city with holiday cheer. We were able to hit up all of the fun holiday attractions downtown while everyone was at work or school. I was able to redo my surgery practicum, saving me from failing this semester of my clinical rotations.

My mind wandered often. I texted Dad off and on, keeping it vague. When we typed an *OK* reply we knew that really meant "no extraterrestrial encounters." Yet. Gabe kept his distance, only because I told Angie I wanted it to be "just us." I knew that excuse wouldn't last long. He had always been like a tumor we couldn't get rid of. His absence was going to rile her motherhood instinct soon.

The ice skating, shopping, and endless television binges helped, but they couldn't push away the fact that I would have to face Gabe this weekend. I told myself I was going to keep drinking to a minimum to keep my head on straight. But how was I supposed to cope with creeper Agent Harris now?

THIRTEEN

Angie's blue satin dress hung from her doorway. Her handheld steamer choked as the hot water clouded around the fabric. The red long-sleeved dress I'd picked out was still in the shopping bag on the kitchen counter. Once again, I was avoiding the social gathering while Ang coaxed me into it.

"Well, we did it." Angie sat admiring her shiny dress. She looked at it with so much pride, and I knew it wasn't the dress. It was the fact that we had both accomplished so much, and we'd lived to tell the tale. Our friend Theresa was holding a Christmas party before the holiday season ramped up. We were all on our own clinical schedules, working part-time to pay the bills. With only one semester of med school left, a small gathering seemed appropriate.

"We're almost there." I stood next to her with my cup of coffee. The dress became a silver screen of flickering memories. Our eyes were drawn to the fabric, but it was really just a place for us to sit and reminisce. So many late nights, so many exams, clinicals—all of it was coming to an end.

"So, you going to profess your love to Gabe tonight?" Angie

chirped, breaking the silence. She looked up at me with an ornery smile, and the corners of my mouth immediately fell into a frown. "He's literally obsessed with you, Jess. Why won't you let the man love you? I mean, good lord, you'd make so much money together, and your kids would be so cute, probably with massive eyeballs . . ." She was about to add more to her fantasy of Gabe and me, but I cut her off. We both did have saucers for eyes, but damn. She always had to meddle.

"He made it pretty clear to me that he wants nothing to do with me after we get our residency applications back," I said blankly.

"Wait, really?" She was taken aback. Luckily, I wasn't lying to her, but I wasn't telling her the full truth either. I was his job. And he was . . . What? My bodyguard/protector/shadow?

"Yeah, he did profess his feelings to me, but he said he had plans to go overseas with Zeke," I answered. It would be fun to start making up lies that he would have to go along with. I would enjoy watching him squirm when I played the undercover game with him. We would see how he liked it. Once we got our residency placements back, he would have to figure out a new lie to tell everyone. How would he fake being a doctor?

Angie gasped. "Gosh. I mean, are you OK?" She knew me well, but she had been trying to get me and Gabe together for years with the only evidence of connection being the laundry room make-out session. It never went further than that, physically. Emotionally, I had fallen in love with my best friend. Last weekend's betrayal ruined all of that for me.

"Jesus, Ang, are you kidding right now? I've done nothing but friend zone that dweeb for the last eight years. He annoys me so much with his high and mighty attitude." Anger started to lace my words.

"You're mean to me sometimes too, but it's because you love me." She threw that sentence out like a dagger to the heart. She was right, but I had to fight back. None of it was real. Even if I did have feelings for him, they were all ripped away when I found out he was actually just an undercover agent, basically a stalker.

"I really mean that meanness to him though. I. Don't. Like. Him. End of story, OK?" I snapped as I made breakfast reservations for the next day on my phone.

"OK. I won't bring it up again." She took the hint and tried to flip the mood back to excited and proud. "We'll be each other's dates. How about that?"

"Aren't we always?" I rolled my eyes.

CHAPTER

FOURTEEN

The little bar our friend Theresa had rented for us was swanky. It was a "speakeasy." Her parents paid her tuition for medical school, so we expected nothing but the fanciest affair. When we knocked on the door to enter, a sliding window opened.

"Password?"

"Shit," I mumbled as I swiped through my phone to find the invitation she'd texted us. Angie looked at me like a little schoolgirl all ready for her first day. It wasn't very often that we got all dressed up. We were usually either doing our clinical rotations at the hospital or lying around in sweats studying and trying to survive. She was still tiny, even with her high-heeled boots on. Her short curly hair was pulled into a low bun, and I wondered if she was going to confess her love to her little friend Harold. She often did this thing where she deflected her love interests and put the attention on me. She was so nice to everyone that it was definitely hard to tell if she was flirting or not. She was also adorable, so everyone was interested in her. In my head I rolled my eyes, but it was an admiring eye roll.

"Residency or bust," I murmured once I finally found the password. *Corny.*

"How cute!" Angie beamed. I let her have this moment. After all, I promised we would have fun. "You look hot! Maybe Gabe will change his mind about leaving the country." She had to get that one in before we entered the low-lit room.

And there he was. It was hard for me not to picture him in his CIA attire. He held a whiskey in his left hand, rolling the ice around.

Weak.

I'd always felt that if you're going to drink whiskey, just drink it straight—feel the burn and move on. If you're going to water it down, may as well make it something fruity. He laughed and bantered with our classmates, and I felt disgusted. He wasn't an agent. He was an actor. I tried my best to hide behind Angie, hoping she would run the night with her extroverted personality. I could ride the waves of her easy conversation, but I couldn't hide behind her physically. I guess I did stand out in heels, towering over her. My red velvet dress was tight, but not too tight. A small pouch and love handles had taken the place where my abs used to be. My thighs rubbed together as I walked, and I felt my bra digging into my right boob. All of the sudden, my skin was on fire and I couldn't hear anything.

Gabe walked across the room. He went to open his mouth—

"You're going abroad in March, and that's why this won't work out. Tell Angie, because I don't want her on my case about our future with large-eyed children and a double-doctor income." I grabbed a soda water off the bar. I asked the bartender to put lime in it so it would look like I was having a good time.

Gabe looked straight ahead, ignoring my comment. I could smell his aftershave, clean like a fresh shower, but spicy. The hairs of my nostrils tingled when I realized I was lingering a little too close. His arm brushed against mine, and I could tell he was using the same strategy that my subconscious had just suggested. He was trying to be cute.

"Are you going to make this hard, or can we act like I'm still helplessly in love with you?" he murmured low through clenched teeth, trying to intimidate me.

"Are you going to give me more information?" I looked up at him as I sucked in the boring lime water. "You know what? Fuck this." My lip curled as I finished my swig. "Shots anyone?"

Gabe's eyes widened, his eyelashes breaking apart from each other right around the edges. Gabe had been sent to "protect" me, but I couldn't help but feel like he was actually here to look for something that was hiding in my past. The bartender poured a combination of whiskey, butterscotch schnapps, and orange juice together in a line of shots. All of us crowded together, grabbing a tiny shooter of the breakfast shot.

"Salud!" I held my glass in front of me, staring directly into Gabe's eyes. I could see Angie behind him, concerned for what would happen next.

"SALUD!" the crowd around me mimicked. Hot alcohol burned my esophagus, and I savored the sweet maple aftertaste. I prayed my pregaming Pepcid would handle that later. Drinks flowed, we ate cupcakes, and Theresa suddenly became the DJ. Angie looked at me from across the room, Harold's arm around her. I gave her a sly smile and mouthed the words, "I'm not drunk." I didn't want to ruin her night with ole Harold because she was taking care of me. I was buzzed, not drunk. I continued to drink my tonic water between rounds of liquor, holding on to enough liquid courage and enough of my self-control to move forward with my plan.

The music started to get louder, and the beat dropped before I could move out of the way. The girls who were in the bathroom formed a stampede as I made my way over to Angie and Harold. I wanted to check in with her before I decided to go in for the kill.

"You know how you said I should say something to Gabe? I'm going to do it. Tonight is the night!" I shouted over the music.

"It took you long enough. Maybe now we can all stop feeling so uncomfortable around you two," Harold said before taking a sip of his drink. I met his gaze with a little bit of anger. "Jess, we all see it," he added and took Angie to the dance floor. Angie giggled, and I realized she was having fun; she would be oblivious to what was really happening when I made my move. I started to walk a little funny, pretending to be a bit tipsier than I actually was. I found Gabe with a group of the guys.

"You know what, Gabe," I slurred. "I feel like the whole 'white coat' thing is ironic, since your actual uniform is black. Don't ya think?" I sneered at him through the circle of men all dressed in their slacks and button-downs. It was such an exciting crew. "Does someone take your tests for you, or do you just happen to be as smart as you are deceitful?" I prodded, waiting for a reaction. Our classmates looked down at the ground, uncomfortable, but clearly not sure whether they should walk away. Was I being a bit spiteful? Yes. But would it help me get the information I needed? Also yes.

His face hardened, Agent Harris showing through his disguise.

Another jab began to escape my mouth, but he cut me off.

"Let's dance!" he shouted over me before I could continue.

He squeezed my arm a little too hard, leading me to the dance floor. I played it cool, not letting him or anyone else know that he was hurting me.

"Tell me what they want." I raised my arms in the air, waving them as the lyrics bounced off the walls and back and forth between all the sweating bodies.

"Please don't do this." His eyes turned doll-like, begging me to stop prying. He fully opened his eyelids, rounding them, letting the only light in the room escape through his pupils. He was scared.

"I deserve to know." My arms wrapped around his neck as I sang along. I could see everyone smirking in the corner of the room. I was finally giving everyone what they wanted. If they only knew that this was an interrogation. "I can make this the most difficult job for you, or you can tell me what's going on. I can help you, Nathan." I played coy. Nathan was his real name, after all.

He spun me around, grabbing my hips, slightly squishing my love handles. With one swift movement he pulled my body against his, with one arm around my waist and the other meeting one of my hands in the air.

"Let go, or I'll tell Angie. And don't threaten me—I know that they need me." I pulled the hand intertwined with mine down to wrap around me and cocked my head back, threatening to kiss him. Instead, I put my lips to his ear. "What. Do. They. Know?"

He flipped me back around to face him, pushing his chest into mine. Whiskey vapors on his breath swirled around with his cherry cigar cologne. The combination hovered in the air in front of us, forming a deceptive mirage. Despite the distracting aroma, I wasn't backing down. His hand was on my lower back. Was it sexual, threatening, or both? He tightened his grip around me, lowering his face to mine.

"Jess, if they find out I told you, I'll lose my job." His desperation took hold of my breath.

"If you lie to me again, you'll lose your job." I lifted an eyebrow. Because if he lied to me again, I would be sure to make him pay for it. His nose brushed against mine. Angie had to be eating this shit up, except she was in the corner swallowing Harold's face.

My eyes didn't falter, and we both sat there as a rapper entered the remix. Gabe's shoulders relaxed. My lips tightened.

"We have reason to believe your mom is still alive," he said in a low tone, the words creeping across my cheek to my left ear. My body went numb. I'd won. So why did I feel even more lost than I had before? It was like I was in rigor, his touch no longer coaxing me forward.

My vision of my mother had been tarnished by the CIA. Every memory I had of her was wiped, twisted, and reimagined. She didn't leave me. She was taken. She wasn't a drunk. She was an agent. And she wasn't dead.

She was alive.

"Jess, please don't do anything stupid." He followed me as I walked to the bar to get another drink. I ignored the audience we had attracted with our little dance scene. My eyes glazed over. I could hear Angie talking to Harold from the barstool on the other side of him. He looked annoyed. He probably thought I'd just ruined his chance to get lucky tonight. Fortunately, Angie was more of a ninety-day kind of gal, so I didn't ruin anything.

My head was spinning even though I had hardly had anything to drink. Angie gave Harold a kiss goodbye. I could see the disappointment in his eyes, but he met her gaze with a sweet smile, knowing she would be thinking of him tomorrow. Gabe played it cool, convincing Angie that everything was fine. It was far from fine. I could not find a mask to hide what I was feeling in that moment. Fortunately, Angie thought it was because I'd just professed my love to Gabe, and his decision to leave to another country had clearly left me heartbroken.

What sucked was that I did have fun. My life was going on like normal, despite all the pandemonium. It disturbed me, though. I couldn't enjoy my success right now with the thought of my mom being lost. Where was she? Did the aliens actually have her, or was she in the next interrogation room on another old couch when we were captured? Was she safe? Was she happy? Were they torturing her? I had no idea if she'd left by choice, or if there had been no other options.

Gabe's eyes held on to me like magnets as I walked out of the speakeasy. I wondered how many times he'd watched through the windows of my apartment. How many times had he followed me home? The lie kept unraveling, exposing different threads that I wasn't prepared to think about. Not only were the aliens watching me, so was the government.

The ride back was quiet. Twinkling holiday decor covered the streetlights and the dead trees, leading our driver home. Wreaths shaped into candy canes and snowflakes alternated. The faster we drove, the faster my eyes tracked from left to right to see them. I imagined Mom on the dirt road. The light pattern hovering over her while the ramp to an unknown ship lowered to take her. Her body was pulled into the machine before it zoomed into the next dimension. The lights were probably the last thing she saw before they took her. What had stopped them from taking me?

When we got home, I left Angie some pain pills, water, and Tums at her bedside. She had done it for me so many times in the past, I felt like I was finally getting to play Santa Claus. Without my usual dosage of alcohol, I was wound up. I pulled up a medieval show about kings, wars, and killing and turned the subtitles on, lowering the volume of the television. Wasn't really sure why carnage and secrets calmed me down before bed, but I needed something to distract me from the thoughts that lingered after my dance floor interrogation with Gabe.

If Mom was alive, I didn't understand why they weren't trying harder to get her back. I knew in my heart the dots were not connecting the way they should. Clearly, I couldn't trust Gabe, but he had more information on what had happened to my mom. If that was true, I couldn't continue to berate him. I had to play nice. The conversation replayed in my head, and the angel on my shoulder smiled as the devil on the other rolled her eyes. I loved hard, but I wasn't *nice*.

My time was almost up with Angie. Tomorrow she would awaken, ready to decide what we would do in the following months. She would be devastated if I went home after we got accepted into our residencies. My stomach ached thinking about breaking the news to her. On the screen, a wedding scene began to play out, but before the couple could kiss and become king and queen, they were all murdered. I had watched this show at least three times. But no matter how many times I watched it, it hurt just as much as the first time. The characters were there to celebrate, only to be stabbed where they ate. Betrayal. I had been betrayed by someone close to me. Gabe and I were close, and he was holding information about someone I'd thought was gone. Now that I had hope that she was alive, it felt like cruel torture. It was a carrot dangled in front of my face, except I was on a treadmill, and I'd starve chasing it.

But my mom was worth starving for.

If I went home, it would force Gabe to follow me there. The thought of him in his stupid suit doing ranch work made me snort. Having Dad nearby would help too; I needed to be around someone else who was in on the secret, because this double life I was living was not sustainable. Disguising my feelings, keeping secrets—it was all too much. My eyes grew heavy, and I made my way to the bathroom, annoyed that I hadn't brushed my teeth and washed my face earlier.

Water ran down my arms as I rinsed. I cringed and rushed to my towel to wipe them before the slithery streams of water could make it to my elbows. My vision was still blurry, and a hazy image of myself looked back at me in the mirror. I paused. I often saw a mix of two people in the mirror, but at that moment I saw a picture of Mom. The older I got, the more she found her way into my features. I noticed my high cheekbones, my large brown eyes, and my prominent nose.

I rubbed my eyes, saddened that I had missed so much time with her. Knowing more about her would allow me to know more about myself. Now that I knew she might be alive, I made it a point to look at my face with a little more determination. I could no longer be reckless.

I needed to save her.

I needed to save myself.

FIFTEEN

ANGIE GROANED FROM HER BEDROOM. I COULD HEAR HER SHUFFLING around the house, blind without her glasses on. I had to admit, I did enjoy not being the hungover mess who had to apologize to everyone the next day. Plus, I was chomping at the bit to grill her about her Harold situationship. Maybe this was why she was always the responsible one. It was kind of fun.

I played around on my phone, scrolling through TikTok. I was stalling. Today was the day we'd promised we would discuss what happened after med school. I didn't want to even think of the next step of my life. It just seemed like so much work to keep moving forward, and on top of that I was walking around every day wondering if I would be abducted. I didn't really see residency going well if I was elbow deep in some- one's stomach, nervous that I would be captured on my walk to the car after surgery. What really irked me was that what- ever I chose to do, there would always be eyes on me. Up until this point I had used substances to push down the feelings of constantly being perceived. They helped me create a mask for each role I played in my life in the city. But the more you wear the mask, the harder it gets to remember who you really are underneath it. I didn't want to use substances anymore, and I didn't want to wear any more masks to fit in. I really wanted to find who I was again.

Right now, the best place to do that was the ranch. I needed my dad.

"This situation is just so wrong," I said, shooting a smile across the room at Angie. When I came into the living room, she was lying in the fetal position on the couch.

"Give me my coffee," she groaned. Her tiny hand reached out as if she was taking her last breaths. I waited to see who she would leave her car to. The Ford wasn't going to last much longer.

"Oh God, you amateur! You really are pathetic, you know?" I was only teasing, but I realized maybe I shouldn't be proud that I had become a professional drinker. She sat up on the couch as I handed over her signature combo of mostly creamer with a splash of coffee. A tiny smile formed on her face, confirming that she was being dramatic.

"Gabe said he isn't leaving after residency."

"Yeah, and what's the situation with Harold? Are you just buddies now, or are we going to pretend that didn't happen?" I said with my eyebrows raised to my widow's peak. She looked at me, unimpressed, which made heat creep up my neck and overflow into my cheeks.

"Dude, you and Gabe were as hot as the telenovelas my grandma used to watch. Spicy! I've never actually seen you dance before. I mean, it looked like you guys rehearsed. I don't think 'friends' move quite like *that*." She looked to the right and pursed her lips into a duck face. How did I explain that that wasn't passion but intense anger? It was a dance of two people who wanted to kill each other but were forced to play pretend.

"Look, Ang, I'm over it. I'm going home to help Dad during calving season when our lease is up in March. I'll stay with you until then, but I'm not really in a hurry to start residency either . . ." I trailed off.

"Wait." She held a finger up to silence me while she processed what I was saying. We were both supposed to go into surgery residencies. We'd planned to carpool together every day to the hospital. We would take turns ordering takeout for each other. We'd live happily ever after. She and Gabe had that in common. They truly thought life was just med school and happily ever after. I was starting to realize that even without all the lies I'd just uncovered, it was much more complicated than that.

"Don't you want me to feel better? I think I just need a break. Dad needs help now that he's getting older, and I can even see if I could do my residency back home. They always need providers out—"

"The place you've been complaining about for the last eight years, Jess? Excuse the fuck out of me if I think that's just a tad bit bizarre!" Her mouth snapped shut. She had more self-control than I did, and I knew that wasn't anger. She was hurt.

"I have to do this for me! I can't keep pushing for everyone else. I'm *exhausted*, and if I keep going like this, there'll be no Jessica Gray left!" My voice had amplified, forcing Angie to cower on the couch. She cupped her coffee with her hand and stared into the empty mug.

"Losing you would be harder than doing residency alone I guess." The words escaped from Angie's mouth in a faint whisper. This was exactly what I was worried about. I hated this too, but there was no other way.

"Didn't Harold say he was thinking about surgery too?" I tried to lighten the mood, returning my voice to sane Jessica.

"I mean, yeah. He's cute and all, but I sure as hell don't want to live with him. We kissed, Jess, we didn't exchange vows."

"A lot can happen in five months, though. You never know!" I sat next to her, nudging her shoulder. Even if there weren't aliens after me—or a weird CIA agent who was oddly attractive yet deceitful at the same time—we were bound to go our separate ways eventually. Plus, after finding out about Mom, I was too far into this. People in situations like this tended to get hurt or get pulled into the chaos. I didn't want to share this burden with my best friend. This was something I had to do on my own.

Through the entire conversation, I'd been ignoring my buzzing phone. I could hear it on my bedside table, vibrating over and over. I didn't have to look to know who it was. Only a real psychopath would quadruple text.

Are you up?

We need to talk.

Noon?

The coffee shop across from the Target.

Before I could answer the text, it buzzed again.

I know you're up, I saw you active on TikTok.

He'd slipped up last night, and I reveled in his screwup. This was the leverage I needed to move forward. I had him by the balls.

Oh were you watch . . .

I deleted my message.

Are all CIA agents so . . .

Deleted again.
I needed to play nice.

See you then.

CHAPTER
SIXTEEN

Gabe's sandy hair was disheveled. I paused at the door of the coffee shop to study him. Finally, I felt like I had some control over the situation. This was the first time I'd ever seen him look so messy. Throughout our entire med school experience, Gabe was flawless, and now I realized he was so flawless because he wasn't *actually* in med school. I was his job, and I was currently a train going off the rails.

The waitress walked to the table with two black coffees, and sweet treats too? He was really feeling it. Nothing in Denver was simple, and I had to admit as much as I loved watching him struggle, the gourmet doughnut that sat at my seat enticed me.

"I got you a crème brûlée something or other. I don't know, I know you like that type of froufrou shit every once in a while. The coffee is black, like you like it." He held his arm out, welcoming me to the table. He didn't even let me sit down before he started groveling, and I loved every minute of it.

"This looks so good." I focused on the crystallized sugar, giving him a chance to form words. I broke apart the hardened coating with my fork, watching the cream ooze out onto the plate. This morning could not get any better. As I took a bite, I noticed he was aggressively running his hands through his hair.

"Dude, get it together. You aren't going to lose your job," I said with my mouth full. He looked up with red eyes, still not speaking.

"Wait, are you hungover?" I pursed my lips, trying to hold in a smile. "My friends are all amateurs. At your age, you gotta double down with electrolytes, antacids, and pain meds."

"Look, I lost my cool. I shouldn't have been taking shots either. And the dancing . . ." He put his face in both of his hands, elbows on the table.

"I understand you're under a lot of pressure, and I know this is weird for you too. But you turned my world upside down and admitted to wiping my memory. Not to mention there are literal UFOs after me. AND my mom may still be alive?" I widened my eyes, making sure he knew who had the right to be freaked out. "I don't really care about your job, I'm sorry. And if you're going to keep creeping on my life, you're going to have to get more comfortable with telling me things. I'm not going to stand by like a good little girl while you fuckers invade my privacy. I want in on the information, and if not, I'll make this assignment a living hell for you. You've known me for how long? I was hell before, imagine me now!" My tone got aggressive. I continued eating to calm my nerves.

"Alright. Alright! But I need to know what your plans are now. If you stay up here, you have to be careful not to draw attention to yourself." He leaned back, relaxing.

"Don't worry. I'm going home. Angie will find out if I stay; she knows me too well, and she's already been on my ass since I fell off my horse." I took a long draw of my coffee while he formulated a plan in his head.

"You realize I'll have to stay there with you, right?" He raised his eyebrows, trying to pick at me.

"Yeah, I do. And guess who's going to work?" I scraped the last of the cream off the plate with my fork, picturing him during calving season. I imagined him in his black suit, riding around on a horse in the middle of a herd of cattle. I let out a laugh.

His eyes darkened.

"Cute. Well, I'll see you, even when you don't see me. Let me know when you're ready to head east. If you don't, I'm sure I'll figure that out too." He picked up his cup, ready to walk out on me.

"Alright. I'm done. But I want to know more about my mom. You know my story, Gabe. You've seen me sloppy drunk cradling the toilet bowl like my life depended on it. Losing her broke me. And now I don't know what to think." My index finger caught a small drip of coffee making its way down the side of my paper cup.

"I really don't know." His jaw was clenched tight. His masseters twitched as he waited for me to keep pushing him. I didn't. "I'm not one of the higher-ups, Jess. I don't know everything. The only reason I know she's alive is because when I read your file . . . Look, I saw that the car accident was all set up. I asked a few questions. Your mom left willingly, and there's speculation that she got something in return for information she had on us." He looked confused, like maybe even he didn't believe what he was saying. He knew as well as I did that it was all a lie.

"But you don't believe that either," I answered, noticing his furrowed brow.

"I have to. I do what they tell me." A quick glimpse of the old Gabe blinked twice to let me know he was still in there. What he'd just told me was the truth.

My brain went into overdrive.

The cash register was behind Gabe. The double doors that led into the kitchen became my point of focus, and the fuzzy pictures from my past began to appear again.

The window overlooked the corrals, the barn, and the mechanic shop. I looked out with a smile, waiting for Mom to bring the remainder of my things up the stairs. We'd decorated the walls of the attic room. My McDonald's toys were packed up in totes. I carefully lined up all of my favorite characters on the counter of my play kitchen. Ronald McDonald gave me the creeps, so I left him in the box.

This was a big step for me, moving my room upstairs. I would be farther away from Mom and Dad, but the space was something I was excited about. I planned all the ways I'd display my toys, all the places I could hang my art. I'd gotten a butterfly releasing kit for Christmas I was dying to set up. My collection of Little House on the Prairie books sat collecting dust, waiting for the next series I would deem worthy to read. My things were scattered across the old, matted carpet, distracting me from my fear. Because every day I got excited about my special space. And every night I found myself back in my parents' bedroom.

I saw things—things that were watching me. I was awakened by sleep paralysis and night terrors. The trembling and shaking was so brutal, I lay awake for hours until I finally fell back asleep. Mom convinced me the eyes I saw watching were only nightmares, figments of my imagination. The green illuminated eyes peered, daring me to come closer yet warning me to stay away. I wasn't convinced that they were part of my dreams.

Each night I settled into my Barbie comforter that smelled like fresh laundry with a tinge of hard water. My eyes were drawn to the point in the ceiling where it met the pitch of the roof. The light from the moon shone through the window, and I focused on the crease, ignoring the quiet. The quiet you could feel always came back.

The two closets on either side of the window were shut when Mom tucked me in. The blackness that pulled at my subconscious told me otherwise. I fought my fear, fidgeting under the covers, untucking the sheets and making sure my entire body was enveloped by my blankets.

It only took one month.

The eyes lurked in the closets, their wooden doors inexplicably open every night.

Every time I went to show my parents, the doors were closed like nothing had happened. The green eyes taunted me.

After that, I moved back downstairs.

"Ma'am, would you like anything else? Your friend paid the tab, but I thought you might want more coffee?" The waitress grabbed my plate from in front of me. My eyes were still locked on the wooden doors behind the counter. Gabe pulled out some cash for the tip and neatly placed it under the napkin holder on our table.

"Yeah, can I get another one of those doughnuts to-go?" I knew Angie would love them. The last gulp of cold coffee went down in one swig. The memory had resurfaced just in time to remind me to put my guard back up.

"You've been gone a while. Is Jess still in there?" Gabe waved his hand in front of my face.

I studied the doors only to see the waitress come through with a paper box loaded with my dessert. I needed more time to sit with my thoughts without Gabe staring at me.

The wrinkled money I dropped on the table landed on Gabe's crisp five-dollar bill. We were right back where we'd started.

I trusted no one.

CHAPTER

SEVENTEEN

FLAILING MALE PARTS AND SCREAMING WOMEN FILLED A HUMID ROOM. The sweat from the abs of a male dancer smeared the soon-to-be bride's makeup. The current setting had me uncomfortable and feeling very awkward, but getting on Gabe's nerves was exhilarating. December through March had been a strange bliss. Medical school was coming to an end. We waited for our residency assignments while we finished up clinical hours and residency interviews. The anxiety was the hardest part to endure. For me, the most difficult part was pretending that I still cared. I knew my journey here was almost over. Sabotaging Gabe until I went home was the only way I could distract myself from the sadness over wasting the last eight years of my life. I would never be Dr. Gray.

I searched the back of the room, looking for Gabe's figure against the wall.

"Who are you looking for?" Angie nudged me.

"No one. I just thought I saw one of our classmates." I had been dragging Angie to the most absurd places in our waiting period. I'd convinced her it was a way for me to let loose, get my mind off the decisions that were coming in March. My routine was so predictable, I realized I was probably lucky someone hadn't killed me yet. I would be the perfect victim. So, to shake things up a bit, I drove different routes. I tried different food, and I even started driving Angie's car. It was all part of my scheme to irritate Gabe.

Every time I brought up an idea I had about my mom, Gabe shot me down. He would walk away from me if I didn't stop nagging at him. When he'd continued to ignore me, I decided to launch my own mission to create turmoil. We'd paid a visit to the drag shows at brunch a few times. Denver had a lot of eccentric places to visit, and I made sure to hit every one of them. I imagined CIA headquarters keeping tabs on our locations and all the explaining Gabe would have to do when he visited locations other than the hospital and my apartment. This was my way of disassociating; this was how I would make it through.

A hand grabbed my arm on the way to the bathroom. I went to scream, but there was already another hand over my mouth.

"You've got to stop." A familiar whisper. My body relaxed when I realized it was Gabe. A small herd of women stumbled into the bathroom following a bride in a tiara.

"Hey, sis, is he bothering you?" The mom of the group spotted us in the corner of the club. Gabe watched me, waiting for me to divert her. I thought about screaming for help. But he was the only way I would find out what happened to Mom.

"Everything's good. He's just practicing his moves for later." I winked back at her. The giggling gaggle of ladies pulled her into the bathroom with them before she could question us further.

"I'm not doing anything wrong." I pulled away from him and walked off. "You're the one making this hard." I only wanted to talk about possible reasons why Mom was taken, or why she might have left. I wasn't making Gabe divulge any more information than he already had. I just needed someone to talk to. He refused.

"You know I can't talk about this, Jess." His shoulders slumped and his head cocked to the side.

"I know. And I can't seem to control my feminine urges." I nodded to the stage full of mostly naked men. Before he could answer, I found my way back to the bathroom.

My new drug of choice was Gabe's frustration.

The indentations from his fingers stung my arm. I rubbed my triceps, trying to make the frustration go away. Instead, it burned hotter. Before I knew it, I was back in my memories.

"Listen to me. You can't tell Dad, OK, sweetie?" Mom held me in the doorway of the foyer. She grabbed my arms, squeezing painfully. Her eyes were black with fear, her pupils sucking in as much light as they could. A single tear rolled from her chin.

"But, Mom—" My whisper was cut off by a sharp hush. Her fingers dug deeper into my arms. Three shadow figures stood outside in the yard, where I had found her. The crunchy leaves rustled as the fall wind stirred up the dead foliage. The breeze burned my lungs and pulled at the hairs on my legs. My night-gown and my hair whipped furiously as the wind picked up.

"I know they look really scary, but these are Mom's friends." She kept talking as I inspected the creatures that did not look very "friendly." Three sets of fluorescent green eyes matched my curious gaze. Only a sliver of the moon shone down onto grayish-blue skin, shiny black suits, and muscles.

"I'll be back before you know it." She grabbed my head, suffocating me with her chest as she took in a long inhale of my scalp. "I love you." Without looking at me again, she walked away.

I never got to say "I love you" back.

"Was that Gabe?" Angie asked. She had followed me to the bathroom of the strip club.

"Yeah," I answered blankly, trying to bring myself back to the present.

"Why is he here?" She stood on her toes trying to see him leave the club. "Is there something you need to tell me?" Her eyes flickered with curiosity and rage. "Are we doing all of this because of him? Are you trying to make him jealous? What's going on? Is he stalking you?" She wouldn't let up.

Shit.

"He's mad that I'm not going with him after our residency assignments. He's been throwing a fit ever since. I think he followed us here to see if I was seeing someone else." I hoped that would stop her from chasing after him. Whether it was the truth or not, she had her radar on him now.

"You're allowed your own personal life. It feels a little possessive. Something about this doesn't sit well with me." She grabbed my hand and led me outside to the car.

"What are you going to do about it? Beat him up?" I laughed, but this time her eyes stayed bright. She opened my door so I could climb into the passenger seat. She waited until I was in and scanned the parking lot. "Ang, do you know something I don't?" I asked when she got into the car.

"You just think you know someone's character. Apparently not." She stared straight ahead as we began to drive toward home.

You have no idea.

CHAPTER

EIGHTEEN

"Ms. Gray, it seems as though orthopedics is treating you well. I'm anxious to see where you're placed in residency." Dr. Graham met me in the changing room after my third successful vertebrae fusion surgery. Since December, I had proven myself again and again. I had completed a few interviews for the final stages of the residency matching process, securing my spot. She was a woman who had a lot of grace, and luckily she'd extended some of it to me when I'd completely blacked out during my first surgery. She was my ticket into my top-choice residency programs. I could even end up working with her.

Not that it mattered.

My phone flashed with a string of missed calls, event notifications, and emails as I opened up my locker.

"Yeah, I guess we'll see," I answered firmly. I was responding to a text from Angie when a call from Gabe interrupted me.

Ignore.

"Just a few more days until you find out, right?" Dr. Graham peeked her head around the locker door, urging me to be more excited. When she saw my face in my phone screen, she understood why I was distant.

"Yeah, sorry. I have some interviews lined up for jobs. I'm not sure how I'm going to stay afloat while I wait for residency to start." Each time I lied, another part of my body seemed to dry up and shrivel away. Soon the only thing left would be the inorganic pieces of bone, an empty skeleton with no sustenance. I'd jangle around like a puppet, the CIA the puppeteers. As I lost myself in a vision of a skeleton performing surgeries and riding horses, my phone started buzzing again.

"You're almost done, kid. I remember those days, but you're so close." Dr. Graham made her way out of the locker room. Her absence gave me a minute to breathe and catch up. I deleted all of the notifications from Gabe. I wanted to ask him about the memories resurfacing, but for some reason Mom's past warning not to tell Dad meant that no one else should know, especially the US government.

An event reminder for Pole Dancing for Beginners popped up next, another one of my plans to mess with Gabe. I'd signed up for it a few weeks ago, Angie giggling over my shoulder. This new side of me was fun for her. Although it was meant to piss Gabe off, it was nice to enjoy these moments with my friend before I had to go back home. A sudden fear danced underneath my skin when I realized this could be my last month with Angie. The fear of the unknown was mischievous, and I could feel it swirling around. I rubbed both of my arms, trying to squash it. It was too quick and found its way back into my stomach.

My workout clothes sat in front of me, reminding me I was late.

When I got to the studio, Angie was already on her way in. We scurried from our vehicles and met on the sidewalk. The hair follicles on my ankles formed spikes, defending my bare skin from the cool winter air.

"Do you think what we're wearing is OK?" Ang looked slightly nervous as she pulled down her spandex shorts. We both wore sports bras underneath our winter coats and ran through the snow in our socks and flip flops.

"We're fine!" I opened the door to let her in.

We were surrounded by women of all ages, all shapes, all colors, and all sizes. No one looked sexy either. Everyone seemed to be dressed in clothes they would wear while getting ready, or regular workout attire. Gabe's black sedan creeped into the no-parking zone out in front of the studio.

Angie's tension melted away when she scanned the room. There was always a level of modesty with her. She never changed in front of me, and I rarely saw her wear clothes that didn't cover her from the neck down. Today she was really stepping out of her comfort zone.

Once the class got going, it felt a little bit like gym class. We were stretching, driving our knees, and doing just about anything but pole dancing. My heart rate climbed, and I realized the cardio aspect of this class had not been properly advertised. By the looks on everyone else's faces, they hadn't signed up for this either.

The instructor laughed and gestured for us to come closer to the poles. She demonstrated a maneuver, wrapping one leg and twirling around. Her chiseled physique squeaked as it twisted around the metal. Our breathing was starting to fog up the picture windows of the studio, and I wasn't sure if I could finish the class after the warm-up.

I was so distracted by the unintended cardio that I'd

forgotten why I was there. We all tried to mimic the instructor, failing miserably. Our muscles didn't grasp the metal like hers and we each slid down the pole with zero core strength.

"Oh my gosh, do you guys see that?" I shouted as we squeaked around the poles. My interruption relieved everyone in the class except for Angie. She was a professional.

She released her body from the pole, landing on the ground and looking in the direction my finger pointed.

"There's some creeper watching us!" I could see a figure in the tinted windows lock eyes with me. The small devil on my shoulder cackled. Gabe's head fell as soon as everyone else turned to look at the black sedan.

"Not again!" the instructor shrieked. Without hesitation she marched outside, rapping on the car door. The glass window that divided us muffled her words.

"I can see you in there! We know you're out here getting photos and videos again!" She tapped on the car window some more. I turned around and one of the other women was on the phone.

"I'm calling the cops. This is the third time this week that we've had to deal with this." She rolled her eyes as she waited for someone to answer. The devil on my shoulder was slapping her knee, but the angel looked at me in fear. If Gabe got caught, I would have to be taken into holding.

A cop car pulled up behind Gabe, chirping its siren.

"Oh hell," Angie exclaimed, hiding her body behind me.

"Ang, your clothes aren't even as revealing as most swim-suits. Calm down." I detached her body from mine, peeling her insecurities off of my sweaty torso. I was focused on the scene escalating outside, but she kept moving with me.

"Jess, can we go? This just feels off to me," she said, holding her arms over her stomach as if she was naked.

"Oh, come on, it's just some creeper getting his rocks off to ladies in their workout attire. He's harmless." I tilted my head to the side and gave her puppy dog eyes to calm her down. She let go of my arm, but whatever was going on with her concerned me more than Gabe.

Gasps from the other women brought my eyes back into focus. The police officer backed away from the door and Gabe exited the vehicle with his hands up. He put his hands on the top of the car as the officer put him in handcuffs. The fog on the windows was starting to clear up. The police officer tucked his chin to speak to his radio. My hands started to melt with sweat, and I could no longer hold on to the pole to stabilize me. I had taken it too far.

When I turned to Angie, I realized she was gone. It was a good thing too, because now Gabe was on full display getting pushed into a cop car. *Shit, shit, shit.* My frantic scan around the room was eliciting looks of concern. From the looks of their sagging stomachs and radiating confidence, these women were absolutely moms. I wished I could run to them with all of my other problems. Their defensive stances let me know they were ready for a fight.

"Sweetheart, your friend went to the bathroom. I think she's pretty upset about our little intruder. We've had several guys coming down here during our classes all week, he just finally got caught." The stranger's eyes darted down to my melted-wax hands.

"OK, class, I'm so sorry about that. Let's get back to work!" The instructor clapped twice as she swung through the door, letting in the cool air from outside. I haphazardly completed the rest of the class, looking to the bathroom every chance I got. Angie stayed in there the entire time.

"Ang, you OK?" I tapped on the door. I could hear shuffling, and I tapped again. No answer. "I'm gonna bust this door down!" I threatened. She immediately opened the door, rushing against me to walk out of the building. Something about today was triggering for her, and I couldn't put my finger on it. Something felt very private about her behavior, and it scared me. We didn't keep secrets. Then I remembered, my entire life was a secret right now.

NINETEEN

My fun was over. I had a best friend who was acting super strange and a CIA agent who was probably going to kill me if his supervisors weren't already on it. The ride home from the studio was silent. Angie didn't speak, and I didn't pry.

She went straight to her room when we got home, and I hid from her in mine to check my phone.

Three missed calls from Gabe, no voicemails, no texts. He answered before it could finish one ring, immediately lecturing me.

"Do you care about anyone but yourself? Honestly?" His voice was short. I was a child getting scolded by my father all over again. The shame and guilt outweighed my hatred for him. The thought of losing access to the only person who could help me find my mom tugged at me. The indentations his hand had made all those months ago seemed to reappear. He was trying to help me. "My job is already on the line, and these little stunts are making everything harder on me. 'Poor Jess, she just does whatever the fuck she wants while Gabe follows her around like a lost puppy dog.' That's been our narrative the whole time I've known you, and now, when you're in more danger than ever, you feel the need to do THIS?!" His breathing was muffled through the phone microphone as we both waited on either end of the line.

"I'm sorry," I managed to squeak out. The pit in my stomach told me what I'd done was wrong, and the small angel on my left shoulder shook her head at me. I couldn't say much more because I didn't want Angie to hear from the other room. "Are you in trouble?"

"No, my boss called in and explained the unmarked car. They said I was on special assignment for sex trafficking. They bought it since there are creepers who sit and watch half-naked women in vulnerable places." His voice calmed; I imagined his jaw muscle relaxing as he spoke.

"You mad at me?" I teased over the phone.

"Yes, I'm fucking mad. You are in actual danger, Jess. You're directly connected to a possible extraterrestrial attempted murder. We have no idea what's going on, and you're gallivanting around town like you're fucking Kim Kardashian or something." The lecture continued, and I realized I had pushed it too far again.

"Alright, alright. I'm heading home soon anyway. You want to come help Ang and I move? I promise I won't do anything stupid until then. Be here Monday?"

"See you then." His answer comforted me, but the guilt continued to eat at me. I pushed problems away; that was what I had been doing since Mom left us. I never wanted to face the issues that hurt me emotionally. It was easier to self-sabotage and replace the feelings with overindulgence in alcohol and bullying. That was why I never went on dates. I didn't welcome any friends other than Angie. I wanted to be alone because it seemed like everyone who got close to me got hurt.

The bed caught my guilt-ridden body. The draft in my room raised tiny bumps on my arms, and I could feel my leg hair catching on the bedding. There hadn't been time to change out of my workout clothes since the debacle. I'd single-handedly ruined Angie's day and Gabe's with my selfish attitude, and it took everything falling apart for me to see that. Why did I do this to myself?

The door slowly opened, and I stood up. A quiet, apologetic, and fully clothed Angie stood in the doorway.

"Sorry about that." She looked down at the floor.

"Everything OK? I've never seen you act like that before." I crossed my legs, and she sat down next to me.

"Everything's fine; that situation was just really overstimulating. Please don't read into it, OK?" Her big brown eyes begged.

"You're sure there isn't something you need to tell me?" This would be the last time I asked, but something just wasn't right. Was she dealing with body dysmorphia? Was she bulimic? Was she sexually assaulted? Was she not comfortable with her sexuality? The clarity I'd gained from giving up my heavy drinking made me think maybe this whole time I was so obsessed with my own mess of a life that I'd been missing clues about Angie. Did I really know her? When we spoke, it was always about my problems. When we went out, it was always my dumbass making a scene. What demons was she battling that she couldn't seem to show me?

There were things I did know. She didn't have a dad. What had happened to him? Her mom had raised her alone, and communication with her was sparse since she left home. When we had breaks in school, she always offered to work more hours at her job. She never invited me to visit her hometown. She always came with me. Eight years had flown by, and today was a hard truth to face.

I was way too self-involved.

"No, I just don't think that was my crowd, and the creeper guy really felt dangerous. That's the first time I've ever felt unsafe since we've lived here. Maybe I'm just having a realization that soon you won't be here with me." She peered at me through her curly bangs.

"Speaking of creepers . . . Gabe is going to come help me pack and move out on Monday." I felt my face pull into a cringe, anticipating an ass-chewing. She wasn't pleased with his "jealous" behavior at the strip club a few weeks ago.

"I can't believe we're saying goodbye." She looked forward, tears welling up in her eyes.

"Our residency matches should be up on Monday. I thought it might be a good distraction from checking our email every five seconds." I kicked my legs at the edge of the bed, wondering if I could ask Gabe more questions once we were back home. Maybe I could figure out whether Mom went willingly. She wasn't murdered. She was running away from something.

"You're right," Angie answered. I felt a slight relief that once I was gone, she wouldn't be a target. She would be safe from getting caught up in the drama that followed me like a rain cloud, striking me down with lightning anytime I was the slightest bit content.

I reached out to hug her. How many times had I mentally broken down in front of her and she'd never judged? Today was odd, but only because she had been holding me up this whole time. It was my turn to be there for her.

CHAPTER
TWENTY

ALL MORNING LONG, I PACED. BOXES AND BAGS LAY SCATTERED ACROSS our apartment. I moved items around the room without actually packing anything. Seeing Gabe face-to-face had my palms sweaty, and having him in the same room as my best friend was just the cherry on top. I had two lies to cover. The first, my attraction toward him, and the second, the secret I was keeping from Angie.

I actually wanted the help, and he told Angie he wanted to tell us both goodbye before he left for Bolivia to volunteer his time. I also felt like if he was there, I would be less likely to fall apart crying. Saying goodbye to our apartment and to Angie was hard.

Angie had been slowly packing for the last two months, taking trips to Goodwill, throwing out old tests she had saved . . . I, on the other hand, had been procrastinating until this day, prepared to just throw everything into unorganized boxes. I had issues getting rid of things, especially all of my old schoolwork. What if I needed those in the future?

The door opened while Angie and I sifted through my junk.

"Hey, guys, it's me." Gabe's voice was in customer-service mode, sounding fake. Angie watched as I rolled my eyes.

"Would you stop it?" she whispered under her breath. Her attitude toward him was forgiving. She had apparently forgotten how he'd followed me to the club the other night. I half expected her to talk shit with me. But it seemed she was back to planning our engagement.

When he walked into the bedroom, I almost didn't recognize him. He had a five-o'clock shadow, and my face turned hot. I hid my embarrassment, pretending to organize things. I pulled out all the clothes I had just put into a box. With my face down, I scanned my eyes to the right, seeing if Angie noticed what I did. She took her elbow and dug it into my side as she folded the shirts I'd left crumpled on the floor.

"Oh, hey, you getting ready to head south? Is the scruff a cultural thing or . . . ?" She was changing the subject, but she was also having fun bringing more attention to his new look.

"Honestly, just got tired of the upkeep." He stroked his face with one hand. "You like it?" He looked down at me.

"Mm-hmm." I kept it short, trying to pull the blood from my face back down to my internal organs. He knew his clean-cut look wasn't going to fit in out east. And the new scruff—I mean, it was *working*. I stood up and hit my head on the end table.

"Fuck!"

"You OK?" Gabe leaned against the doorway. He knew he looked good, but he would say he did it to blend in when we moved to the country.

"I'm fine! Let's start loading some of these in the back of my pickup before we get snowed on." I waited until he grabbed a box to further examine him. His grooming didn't seem as clean. Stubble protruded from his chin and cheeks, and some of his bangs fell over his forehead. The dark facial hair contrasted his light green eyes. I couldn't keep up with the different versions of him.

For the last couple of months, I'd been thinking of all the time we'd spent together, all the laughs and the late-night study sessions. He was my *friend*. Gabe and Angie were my support system through school, and I wouldn't have finished without them. Whether I was having a mental breakdown because of all the socializing and the overwhelm or being an outright bitch to other professionals, they were there to back me up. I had zero control over my emotions sometimes, especially when I was overwhelmed. But they knew that regardless of my very rigid way of thinking, I always had their backs too. And yes, I'd pushed him away. I'd never wanted a relationship because, truthfully, I couldn't handle a relationship. But then again, was that all just part of his act?

"A little help here?" Gabe gestured at the door with his eyes. He had a huge box of my plastic dishware and kitchen supplies. He was pretending that the semester party, the meeting at the coffee shop, and that whole part where he kidnapped me hadn't happened. But what about his crush on me? Had that really happened? All the times he helped hold my hair while I puked into disgusting college apartment toilets. Was that part of the job description?

I followed him through the doorway, working to keep up with him as I carried hangers full of clothes.

"Slow down!" I whispered. He pretended not to hear. "Gabe," I tried again. He shoved the door open with his body, turning to face me.

"What's up?" he answered with a blank face. When I looked him in the eyes, they were lifeless. The emotion seemed to drain from him every time Angie was out of sight. The minute she entered the room, fun, playful Gabe acted his way through the apartment. He was making me pay for the torment by turning his body from me, looking through me instead of at me. He put on a charade for her, but I got nothing. I searched for the words to get him to make this less grueling.

Back in my room, I slammed bags around the space, shoving in random items that would be sure to make a lot of noise. I thought I was portraying anger, but it was really my sadness. Because in one day, I was saying goodbye to my best friend, and I was accepting the fact that Gabe was just a transaction paid for by the CIA. I took any sense of friendship we had left and flushed it down the toilet.

I had one more trip down to my pickup before we would be ready to go. Gabe and Angie were doing a walk-through to make sure we didn't leave anything behind. The air was cold, and I realized all the sweat I'd worked up going up and down the stairs was now making me shiver. I clenched my teeth together, avoiding the inevitable. When I went upstairs, it meant goodbye.

I locked the pickup door before shutting it with a creak. As I slammed it shut, a loud snap accompanied it.

Snap! Snap!

Two more.

I recognized the sound of gunshots, something I hadn't heard in the center of the city before. I was used to waiting for the bullet to makes its way through yards and yards of prairie before smacking its intended pest on the ranch. These snaps were confined, and they had come from my apartment building.

Angie.

My body went from human to machine, vibrating with thumping anxiety. I could hear my heart in my ears as I ran up to my apartment. The metal stairs clanged, and when I got to the top of the stairs, I dialed 911. My thumb hesitated over the green call button as I slowly opened the door.

There in front of me, a man lay face down on the ground, and on top of him . . .

"Angie?!" I screeched.

She had him on the floor with one foot on his neck, her tiny hands prying his arm back as he groaned. I rushed into the living room, shutting the door behind me. Gabe's gun had been kicked across the room, and I picked it up, unsure who to point it at.

"She's—" Gabe tried to squeeze the words through his larynx. Her small snow boot constricted the words. "One of them," the whisper squeaked out. She pried his arm harder, causing him to wriggle around. It was like someone tickling a small child who couldn't escape.

"I think we need to talk," Angie said as she used an extension cord to tie Gabe's hands and feet.

TWENTY-ONE

"Put the gun down." Angie broke the silence. The gun barrel hovered back and forth between the two of them.

Cock the hammer, Dad's voice said in my left ear. The only handgun I had ever shot was a .22 revolver. I'd pinged a few aluminum cans, but this was slightly different. I didn't need to cock the hammer. All I had to do was pull the trigger. And my target was much larger than an aluminum can.

Angie hoisted Gabe up into a chair, ignoring my shooting stance. He tried to speak, but his words were garbled since there was duct tape across his lips. I hesitated, looking at the counter where I could set down the gun. If I shot her, I would be shooting my best friend. If I shot him, I would be murdering a CIA agent.

I noticed there were two phones on the counter, along with Gabe's badge. She knew.

"I think now that he isn't going anywhere, we should all have a little chat." Angie's tone went from bubbly and sweet to very harsh. Her shoulders seemed to broaden with authority.

Her cheek bones and her chin appeared to have been chiseled with a new look. The position of power suited her. This was not Angie.

"What the fuck is going on?! She's one of them? What does that mean?" I begged, that damn frog kicking on my uvula again. I decided to keep the gun, pointing the barrel down at the ground, ready to aim if needed.

"I think you know what it means." Angie picked at her hairline with her fingers, peeling a wig off to expose a bald, gray head. My teeth were about to break under the pressure of my anxious jaw. With both hands, she started picking again, except it was like she was trying to peel dead skin from her forehead. I had done this many times after a sunburn, but this wasn't dead skin. It wasn't even *her* skin. A layer of silicone suctioned from her face. The same gray color became visible, iridescent with blueish green undertones.

Gabe's eyes needed a cartoon sound effect; they grew to the size of his face, masking all of his other features. I was not in shock, only in awe. I was not surprised, I was validated. The memories that had been resurfacing were real.

And there was something so strange about a person, a thing, looking so similar to a human yet so different. It struck me as peculiar, but it seemed to strike Gabe in an entirely different way. Probably because he didn't know as much as I did. The look on his face confirmed that the CIA hadn't told him as much as they could have. He wasn't keeping things from me. He was in the dark, and he was completely terrified.

Just when I thought the reveals were over, Angie pulled down her eyelid. A brown disc blobbed onto the pad of her index finger, and there they were. The green eyes that had been haunting me had never left. Fish scales in the sun, soap bubbles reflecting summer light . . . Her skin mesmerized me.

"I think you get the picture," she continued in her new, powerful voice. "I'm going to do the talking. From the sounds of it, you idiots already filled her head with lies," Angie barked at Gabe. Her commanding tone pulled me back to her green eyes, shining and fluorescent like we were in a room with black lights. Gabe sat with his arms behind his back and his legs tied to one of the only chairs we had left in the apartment. I was still in shock at how someone so little could so easily over-power a six-foot-three man. Angie gave me no time to speak, and she ignored the gun in my hand.

"My full name is Angela, and I am from Veritan, a planet a few galaxies over, in the Lacertus galaxy. We've been keeping a close eye on you since your mom took residence. When you relocated to a more populated area, your mother sent me to stay close to you. You were much easier to watch when you were in the rural regions. She didn't feel comfortable bringing spacecrafts into such a big city." Angie paused, kicking Gabe when he mumbled under the duct tape.

"I knew she wasn't taken." My fingers slipped from the gun at my side, and I let it drop to the floor in defeat.

"That's what these bastards wanted you to believe. Your mom was a CIA agent on Project CORE, and in 1990 your mom found Veritan and met my parents. The United States had been searching for other planets that could sustain human life. They were working on a deal with the planet that neighbors us, Mendax, known for their mining. The naïve Americans made friends with them immediately. There are sufficient amounts of sunlight and oxygen available there for life-forms like your-self. Your mom's job was to make the deal go smoothly. You would have a backup planet to use as refuge if things went wonky on Earth, and in exchange, the US would give them oil. But we've been fighting this planet off for years because they don't honor their deals. They take from whoever they can, and they never give anything in return. They will bleed a planet dry. They will enslave you."

The frog was unleashed. My body convulsed as I started to cry. No more holding back.

With no hesitation, Angie continued on. "Your mom was on a mission when she was intercepted by one of our ships. We were able to show her our history—thousands and thousands of years of fighting to defend our planet from the Mendaxians. The United States fell into a trap that wasn't even set up for them. We had no idea of Earth's existence until your missions led you to our galaxy." As she finished her sentence, I saw frustration in her eyes. The way she spoke, it was as if this had all happened just yesterday.

"When she came back from the mission to tell the United States government, they didn't believe her. She continued to push back, begging them not to make the deal. She was asked to leave, and her memory was wiped. For some reason, it never worked on her . . ." She trailed off.

"Like me," I finished her thought.

"Yes, like you. She met your dad shortly after and asked him to move out to the country. We had been waiting to hear from her about whether the deal was made, and when we heard nothing, we came searching. The government knew something was up, and when she wouldn't stop communicating with us, they attempted to take her out. That was when Veritan stepped in."

I stayed silent. When I thought things couldn't get any weirder, they did.

"We took her with us, hoping to formulate a plan to save Earth. You are one of the only planets left that can help us fight the Mendaxians. Veritan is a planet of highly trained military-ready beings. We've had to be to keep our people safe. But our resources, our numbers, and our hope are starting to dwindle.

Our protective force field repels them, but it's only a matter of time before that isn't enough. Soon, we won't be able to fight Mendax off anymore. We need you as much as you need us." She paused, seeming to question whether she needed to slow down. I nodded in understanding. I wanted to know more. "She thought you'd be able to live a normal life, but we soon realized you remembered. We also saw the suits keeping tabs on you. They were using you as leverage to taunt your mother. They were using you to taunt us." She stared into Gabe's eyes.

This story answered questions I didn't know I had. It filled the blanks that the CIA had left out. Mom wasn't a strung-out drunk—she was trying to be a hero. For a few moments, Ang watched as I took the information in. My tears started to dry, and I found myself in Gabe's eyes. They were full of fear and confusion. He was a liar, but was he that kind of liar? Mom had been trying to protect me this whole time, and that was a story I could believe. I was teetering, unsure whether to trust Gabe or Angie, but I knew one thing for certain: my mom was no liar.

"So, what do we do with him?" I pointed, resembling a grade school kid tattling on her playground bully. Gabe squirmed beneath his restraints. The narrative Angie had told comforted me more than the story I'd heard in a concrete holding cell. I wasn't being restrained or taken to a secret lair this time. Angie was an alien, but I felt like I could get over that.

"We have to play along. *He* has to play along. When you told me you were going home for a while, I knew it would be a perfect opportunity to get in touch with your mom, but I found out this little dweeb was in on it the whole time. You both started acting up at the Christmas party, and when he showed up at a strip club . . ." She looked at Gabe as she spoke. He rolled his eyes at me, like it was my fault we were being surveilled by another life-form. "They've been monitoring our airspace, watching us closely. If we can get him to play nice, there may be a chance we can make contact with your mom," she said with hopeful eyes. The room went silent, and I found myself trying to picture what Mom would look like so many years after her "death." She would be a stranger, and part of another planet's community.

We all sat in the empty apartment. I was stuck in the middle of my two best friends, one of them a liar, and the other an alien. I found my coffee still on the counter and took the ceramic mug in my hand. Both of my friends stared as I popped it in the microwave.

"I need a minute." My awkwardness still made them uncomfortable, no matter how long they had known me. Though they were used to it, the way I handled situations still confused them. This time I chose to cry, zone out, and drink coffee until the last drop was gone. When that moment passed, I would be ready to move on to the next item of business. I found another chair, crossed one leg over the other, and began to bounce my foot. The rhythm started to soothe me along with the hot coffee, and I could feel them impatiently waiting while I found a point of focus in the room.

"Can you stop breathing like that?!" I screeched at Gabe. The duct tape over his mouth was revealing a very unattractive deviated septum. The loud whistles and faltering breath would be my breaking point, and I may or may not feel obligated to put a bullet in him. Angie joined me, facing her body toward Gabe but settling next to me comfortably.

"That's why you never undressed in front of me." I stated it as a fact. "And you never had any romantic relationships," I continued. She didn't acknowledge me. When her eyes finally met mine, I realized why she never got wrinkles. The lack of blemishes, the perfect skin—it was all fake. The green eyes were warm, not piercing. The picture I had in my mind when I saw aliens wasn't this. She wasn't scary or weird; she was beautiful. Her features were still the same under her human-like mask, including her round face and her big smile. Makeup artists would kill for such a stunning canvas. They may not be so keen on the fact that she didn't have normal ears. They were small, raised crescents on the sides of her head. The almost invisible slits that kept opening and closing right behind those crescents made me curious about the way her planet, Veritan, looked. *Would it be rude to ask?*

It had all been there in front of me, just like Gabe. They weren't good at hiding who they were, I was just terrible at paying attention to anyone but myself.

"I know you probably need more time, but we don't exactly have any left." She broke the silence, putting her gray hand on mine. The texture felt waterproof, and the spaces between her fingers were filled with translucent webs. *How did she hide those?*

"I don't know if I fully trust you, but I don't think I have a choice." I stood up from my chair. My eyes came back into focus as I scanned the room. We only had a few bags left.

"You really don't," Ang agreed, and we both noticed Gabe was watching the encounter with wide eyes. His fear scared me. The fight-or-flight impulse may force him to run to his buddies in suits. I loathed him, I loved him, and now I felt bad for him. He was just another pawn in the game the government was playing. The fewer people that knew what was going on, the more people they could trick. They could continue to keep their secrets and give away our resources to another planet. They were going to bleed us out like a pig at slaughter.

As Angie neared, he tried to scream under his duct tape. She giggled at the sight of his fear. My angel seemed distressed for him, but the little devil on my other shoulder smiled, wondering how he liked the interrogation and the slap in the face of secrets being kept from him.

"Should we head east?" Ang looked at me the way she always had, her teeth now even brighter against her skin and pearly blue lips.

"Let's go." I shrugged my shoulders.

What else am I going to do?

CHAPTER
TWENTY-TWO

"Scream and I'll shave that cute little beard of yours with a rusty butter knife," Angie said under her breath. Her tiny hand clasped Gabe's, their fingers intertwined as if they were dating. His face was still red from the duct tape. From the terrified look on his face, it was pretty clear he knew that no human life-form was going to win against Angie. Now that I knew the truth, her disguise looked like a bad Halloween costume. Her eyes were way too large, and her torso way too long. It was similar enough to what a human *should* look like, but once you saw it, you couldn't unsee it.

Without his gun, Gabe was no match for her. The way she'd taken his 200-pound body and thrown him to the ground when she tried to untie him confirmed she was not from this Earth. I walked behind them, contemplating whether or not I should just make a run for it. But why? Regardless of whether I believed either one of these psychos, I was in too deep. One of them or their colleagues would soon find me. Dad's safety also depended on me. I wasn't going to risk his life by doing something stupid.

We were going to head east out to Dad's place and see if we could talk some more with less of an audience. The neighbors next door had already called the police, and we told them someone set off some old fireworks. Kids doing stupid stuff in apartment complexes wasn't a surprise, and thank God they bought it.

"Let's just move these boxes over to your buddy's new ride." Angie used her eyes to point at the Ram 2500.

"Whose vehicle is that?" I asked, confused.

"Looks like the CIA gave Gabe an upgrade! Guess they wanted him to fit in with the shitkickers out in the country." Angie giggled. I couldn't help but feel like nothing had happened. She still seemed like my friend, only a little more confident and a lot more badass.

"I don't feel like that's very discreet, but I guess if we hit snow, we won't have to worry about my shitbox making it home." I started laughing, trying to hide my nerves. One part of me wanted to play it cool, but the other was worried that I would die in the next few hours. She would probably just shoot me and leave my body to be scavenged by coyotes. She would be whisked away by a fancy spaceship, and voila, no more Jessica and Gabe.

Angie turned to face Gabe. "Where are the keys?" she ordered. I was always one step behind her. She must have already frisked him before we got downstairs.

"It's a coded door," he said with ease. His face stayed blank, and I couldn't tell if he was scared, upset, or formulating a plan. If he decided to run, I didn't know if I would go. Angie yanked him toward the driver's side and forced him to input the code.

The lock clicked, and Angie forced him through the driver's side door. His large stature made it difficult to make it over the center console into the back seat. Once he was in, she immediately set the child lock. His shoes scraped over the front seat, scuffing the new leather. She instructed me to stand on the passenger side to make sure he didn't make a run for it. I waited for her cue to enter the front seat.

"They do realize that most people don't actually drive this nice of a vehicle where I come from, right?" I asked, half hesitant to break the ice in our new situation. No one replied. The uncomfortable feeling made my jaw clench down again. The engine rumbled and we made our way out of the city, finding a road more fit for a one-ton diesel.

Once I saw more pasture than I did housing developments, I tried to dissipate the tension that clouded the inside of the cab. Angie had the seat all the way forward, barely able to reach the pedal thanks to her size. I sat with the two people I'd thought I knew like the back of my hand, and I couldn't find the right words to say. The space where I used to feel comfortable felt more like a failed blind date. As I focused on my words, the sound of my breathing got louder, and I wondered if they could hear. I focused on the screen in front of me. The forecast, the map home, and the music on the radio all broadcasted on the newly upgraded pickup. All the gadgets distracted me, and I forgot what I was going to say.

"Jess, just save your questions for when we get there. I don't feel like repeating everything to your dad. I'm also not sure how he's going to take this. Remember, he still doesn't know your mom is alive," she said without looking away from the road.

We hit our first cattle guard, and I made a mental note of all the questions I had for her. I wanted to make sense of the past, and it sounded like it would determine my future. The email notification for our residency applications had sat unopened on my home screen for the last three hours. Our plan to create a distraction had worked.

I'd made it into the orthopedic surgery residency. With one swipe, the email was gone. With one swipe, that part of my life was over. Disappointment seemed to be my first reaction, then some pride, and finally relief. Because becoming a doctor had always been a way for me to find my purpose in life—to fill the void. Now that I knew Mom was still out there and that I was part of something much bigger than myself, it seemed that my prayers had been answered.

The dirt roads jostled my body into a nice, dazed state—my comfort zone. Since meeting the CIA agents, the memories had festered, emerging from their appropriate hiding places. I let myself drift into the past.

The Big Dipper was prominent in the sky above me. Grass tickled my ears, and the smell of summer was fermenting. Long prairie grass and fragrant sagebrush made even the scent of horse manure pleasant. Mom had died three years ago, and I spent these summer nights looking for her in the sky. Dad never took me to church, but it seemed like God—or whoever took care of the dead—was up there. I figured Mom was too. She drank a lot, but she wasn't a bad person. Dad's sitcoms were muffled by the screen door, and I found comfort in this nightly routine.

Our border collie zoomed past my ear, breaking my gaze from the stars. Yaps and growls interrupted the comforting buzz of the television. Annoyed, I sat up. Snuffy was a working dog; she chased cattle, herded chickens, and acted as a companion.

But bark? Never.

She sped back and forth across the front yard, ignoring my presence. Every few laps she would stop and stare. The dirt road leading up to our home was broken up by a fence to define our house from the rest of the ranch.

Yellow eyes stared at us beneath the cattle guard, the grated piece of metal that kept animals from entering our yard.

They peeked through the grates, never moving. Snuffy continued to lose her mind, whining at the end of every one of her yapping episodes. Bobcats, rabbits, coyotes, badgers . . . They had all made their way to and from our house at times. I wasn't afraid of them. But the summer air no longer felt warm, and the sweet smell of vegetation disappeared. My fear was cold, and the aroma of an ice box full of dust blew away my calm evening.

It was watching me.

"Knock it off!" Dad snapped at her. His chair creaked. He had fallen asleep. Snuffy cowered, but she continued pacing back and forth. Her shoulders hunched forward, and she bared her teeth with each pass she made in front of the chain-link fence. The eyes were gone, but I kept my gaze locked on the blackness beneath the metal grate. Snuffy postured forward, still focused on the road. The cool fear bit at my ear, and it spoke to me.

Run.

The eyes flashed again, farther up the road this time, watching me before they disappeared. I raced toward the house. The metal door handle stuck under my thumb, my grip rattling its hinges. I almost pulled the door out of its frame before I realized Dad was watching me with confusion.

"What on earth are you doing?" He slowly pushed his side of the door latch. The door squeaked open with ease.

"I feel like something is really wrong," I said, walking back inside. I took one more look before shutting off the porch light.

"It was probably just a bobcat! Get to bed before you give yourself nightmares," he answered.

Do bobcat eyes glow?

Back in the present, we were almost home, with one more

cattle guard to cross—the same one the eyes hid under in my distant memory.

"Do any of the Veritans have yellow eyes, or are they all green like yours?" I asked.

"We all have eyes like mine. Why?" Angie answered blankly as she made her way into our circle drive to park.

"No reason," I replied, because I knew the answer. I knew that even though the good guys were watching me, the bad guys were too.

Mendaxians.

CHAPTER
TWENTY-THREE

WHEN WE GOT TO THE HOUSE, DAD WAS GONE. THERE WERE 500 head of pregnant cattle about to be thrown into active labor because of the change in temperature and barometric pressure. Snow came in sideways in eastern Colorado, and the drifts had already started to form.

"I told your boss you made it safely to your destination." Angie was the boss now, and her tone was matter-of-fact. I could tell it bothered Gabe to lose control, and I was secretly enjoying the two-against-one dynamic we now had going. I stopped in the foyer of the house and started to change my shoes and add layers of warm clothes. Angie found some of my extra stuff and followed suit. She was no stranger to ranch work, especially since she never had anywhere to go during her breaks. Now I knew that it wasn't just because home was too far, it was because it was *really* too far. Like, outer space far.

"What, they decked you out with a new pickup but they didn't give you any work clothes?" I scoffed at Gabe. He was standing at the door in his preppy outfit. He wore jeans and a plaid flannel shirt. Instead of a cowboy, he looked more like the hometown love interest in a Hallmark movie. Maybe a lumber-jack type of vibe? Angie and I wore faded, lined denim jackets, and over those another layer of brown canvas coats. Lined muck boots and worn jeans were appropriate. Mainstream media only portrayed cowboys when they were horseback, but they hadn't let Gabe in on the fact that most of the time we were on foot, knee-deep in cowshit. "Dad has some stuff in there that should fit you." I nodded to the closet next to the dryer. Dad wasn't as "built" as Gabe, but at least they were roughly the same height. "Grab some of those bibs too in case we have to go break ice."

I was in my safe place, something Gabe wasn't used to. My confidence skyrocketed, and the new power duo that Angie and I had created felt like a strong coffee on an empty stomach. It was completely unhinged—an absolute jolt to the system. It was a step up from having a celebrity as a best friend. My friend was out of this world. Literally.

Calving season was always difficult and tiring, but there was something special about getting to help new life into the world every March. When I met Angie, she had quickly become a part of the tradition. Gabe had never been involved in my way of life, and the defeated look on his face was another confirmation of how upsetting it was for him. Angie shared something with me that he didn't, and the jealousy that radi-ated from his large build was palpable. I considered Angie my family; even though she had lied to me, there was something about her that made me trust her. I didn't feel that way about Gabe anymore. I knew his feelings for me, but he was in bed with the wrong side, and I just knew it.

The horses shielded themselves from the wind in their corrals. The metal door on the barn slammed repeatedly. I remembered the winter weather warning last night on the news. The white speckles covered the state of Colorado, but near the Kansas border, it was concentrated. I had been so distracted by the thought of saying goodbye to Ang that I didn't anticipate a possible blizzard.

Angie holstered Gabe's weapon and kept his phones inside the breast pocket of her coat. We made our way to the shop, and I had a feeling the alien backstory was going to have to wait.

Two calves lay on an old carpet in front of the woodstove. Water soaked into the concrete where the snow melted off their newborn hair, and I wondered how many more had dropped. Once again, this place had a way of distracting me from what was really happening, and I found myself in work mode, ignoring the fact that I was surrounded by liars. I directed Angie to fill two bottles with warm water, and I found an open bag of formula. We both shook the massive bottles, mixing the white powder.

The Chevy was gone, which meant Dad was still out and about. I felt guilty for how little I'd worried about him while I was off at school. Now that I was home witnessing the elements firsthand, I felt like he needed a partner. What happened if his pickup broke down, or if he fell? Or what if one of the bad guy aliens abducted him? That may have been a more concerning thought at this point.

Both calves defrosted from the inside out. As they drank the milk, warmth seemed to circulate through them, breathing life back into their stiff bodies. Angie handed Gabe the bottle, not letting him have too much time to himself. I wondered how long this nonsense would go on, or if it would ever end. It was reassuring to have more control of the situation, and to learn more information about my mom. But the tension between my best friends would get old eventually.

When I heard the Chevy rumble over the cattle guard, a sense of relief washed over me. I popped the nipples off of each bottle, preparing to rinse them. In the corner of my eye, I saw Gabe petting one of the little Black Angus heifers. When he did simple things—tasks that had nothing to do with aliens, or the government, or saving the world—he was just Gabe. At the same time I'd found out he was an agent, I'd also realized how much I had fallen in love with the man I thought I knew.

For a fleeting moment, my heart twinged, reminding me it still existed. His attempt to be a part of something I'd worked so hard to shut him out of felt nice, but it also hurt. The veins and tendons moved beneath the skin of his hands as he scratched behind the floppy ears of the newly defrosted baby. The sweet, green eyes I knew were soft and complemented his new scruff and rugged collared coat.

But the truth of my life was unraveling quickly. The truth was, I was in love with a man who couldn't be trusted. He was one of *them.*

Angie cleared her throat louder than necessary.

"I can still look," I hissed as I poured soapy water out of each bottle. Now that she didn't have to act anymore, her attitude toward him had changed entirely. She was even more protective of me than before. She was lethal.

A door slammed outside the shop, then another. My brow furrowed, and I noticed Angie mirror my confusion.

"Did you send more agents?!" I snapped my head around to Gabe. He stood from his squatted position, and before he could answer, Angie pulled her gun from her hip. I could see Dad's lanky stature through the window, snow pelting him as he walked in. My eyes darted back and forth between the door and the tip of Angie's 9mm pistol. When I was a kid, I was taught not to point guns at people, and this new normal was getting out of hand. My warmed heart went into overdrive with adrenaline. What if they were holding Dad hostage?

Suddenly my warm clothes were no longer comforting, and the sweat stuck the fluffy fibers to my skin.

Angie, please don't shoot.

There was another figure behind Dad, probably Angie's intended target. He slowly opened the door, his silver mustache coated with melting snow. His smile indicated he was happy until he scanned the room to find Angie's gun pointed at him.

"Angie?" he asked, confused. Whoever was behind him walked into the building with their head down. It was a woman. The wet milk bottles still occupied my useless hands, and Gabe rushed in front of me.

"I—" Dad raised his hands in reaction to the gun, and when the woman looked up, Angie lowered her weapon.

"Rosa," Angie said, gasping.

"Jessie?" The woman smiled.

"Agent Rodriquez," Gabe said seriously.

"Mom?" I managed to get out. Her black hair was tinseled with gray, wrinkles formed between her eyebrows, and her eyes were cold and lifeless.

She came home.

CHAPTER
TWENTY-FOUR

"Jess, have you stoked the fire? It's going to be a long night," Dad exclaimed as he shut the blizzard outside. All of us sat staring at each other. Once again, I was in a room full of people I didn't know. Once again, I was looking into the eyes of a person who knew me better than I knew myself.

The rest of the room waited for my reaction. At this point they were probably just as worried about my reactions as I was. My reflex was somewhere between crying and stabbing someone. The stranger approached me slowly, her eyes softening with each step. The agent I'd never met melted into the mom I knew. The woman I'd seen so many times before in the mirror was standing in front of me. Mom was alive. Mom wasn't an alcoholic. Mom didn't abandon me.

"Jessie, sweetheart. Come here." Her clothes, still stiff from the cold, crushed into my warm body. Before I could stab anyone, tears started flowing instead. Crying was becoming a regular thing for me, and I guess it was better than the other option. The more crying, the less alcohol. Her face was in my neck, and I could smell the oils in her hair. The scent was earthy and familiar. I was back on the couch cuddling her when I was little. She was still my safe space. She inhaled and squeezed harder until we both realized everyone was watching. Sniffles were the only noises other than the dwindling fire, and we broke away from the hug.

"You're here," I managed to grumble out through the mucous buildup in my throat.

"I'm here," she replied.

The door of the stove creaked as Dad added more wood to the fire. The new logs fell on top of glowing embers, scattering small flecks of ash around the newly added pieces. There was so much conversation around me, but I heard nothing. My focus switched back and forth between the hot stove and the sleeping calves. It took all of me not to stare at my mom, not to resent her for leaving, not to pounce on her for ruining our lives. I was supposed to be a new doctor right now. Instead, I was dealing with mommy issues and aliens.

But it wasn't her fault.

The buzzing around me quieted. My eyes recognized the blurred figures my mind had so easily blocked out. My skin could sense the eight sets of concerned spheres prying at my disassociation. I wanted to stay gone. I wanted to disappear and forget any of this ever happened. I thought I had unmasked my issues a long time ago, but now, there was nothing holding back my instinct to run away and hide from the world.

"I'm sorry I called you by your nickname. I just . . . I hardly ever called you—" Before she could go on, I cut her off.

"You hardly knew me at all." I continued staring at the stove. The door was now shut, and I found a spot where soot had powdered the doorframe gray in color. The room was now even quieter, and everyone danced around how to talk to me. I knew she was alive, but actually seeing her, having confirmation that she'd been alive this whole time and had no problem leaving me—that was something I wasn't prepared for. Thinking she was dead and not knowing she was out there had been much easier.

"I know this is hard for you, but your mom had no choice, Jess. Right now, we don't really have a choice either. If something isn't done soon, they're going to hurt us. They might take out the entire human race . . ." Dad trailed off, his eyes finding the same spot on the stove. It hadn't taken long for Mom to catch him up on most of the details. He was taking the information a lot better than I was.

Angie, the one who knew me the best, stayed silent. She anxiously cleaned the shop that hadn't been cleaned in years. Her small body zoomed around in the background sorting nuts and bolts, sweeping up the concrete floor.

"I didn't know any of this." Gabe's voice brought everyone back to attention. I looked up, getting ready to fire back. I had no patience for his lies. Before I could put together a snide remark, he answered his own statement. "All they told me was that there were alien life-forms that were dangerous, and they took one of our agents. I was sent to protect you, Jess, I swear." Those desperate green eyes stared into mine, pulling me out of my disassociated state. Tears of anger welled in my eyes, and I unleashed a convulsive cry. It was a cry that didn't need comfort. It was a cry that everyone in the room felt. The pain and the overwhelm of every event leading up to this one had caught up with me, and I could no longer hold it together. There was no room in my brain for a single ounce more of information, and the overflow burst out as a river of tears.

I growled in anger, clenching my fists. I remembered everything. Everything.

Feet scuffled around me as Angie tried to discreetly get Gabe out of the shop and Dad followed. I huffed in and out rapidly, closing my eyes in frustration. Mom wrapped her arms around me, but her short limbs were no match for my vibrating body. The muscles of my diaphragm hiccupped over and over, and I held my stomach, trying to convince it to stop. She hugged me even harder, providing pressure I didn't know I needed.

I don't know how long we sat there together, but I eventually ran out of energy and tears to cry. Snot and drool covered my face, and my eyes were almost swollen shut.

"I never stopped watching you grow up, and I'm so sorry that it happened this way. I didn't know that you would reject the memory wiping like I did. I tried my best to protect you from this mess I uncovered, but I guess it's hereditary." She moved in front of me, and my eyes caught on her smile lines. I wondered what she could have smiled about knowing she'd left her family here. "We have a lot of catching up to do, and I know this isn't ideal, but if we don't figure this situation out, we may not have a world to catch up in," she added. In the aftermath of my episode, the salt from my tears started to dry on my face, making my skin feel tight and uncomfortable.

"The good news is, Gabe has become your friend, and he's exactly the leverage we need to get the government's attention. You've done such a good job, Jess. You didn't even know what was going on, but you handled this with more composure and skill than any normal person. Anyone else would have blabbed to the wrong person and ended up in the looney bin." Her white teeth shone with pride as she talked about the last few months of my life. I knew it wasn't her fault; it would just take a while to get over all the lost time. None of it was fair, but what was in this life?

"I just don't understand how more people don't know this is happening. How has this gone on for so long? Why did only one person stand up? Why did it have to be you?" I said with a shaky voice. I had to clear my throat.

"We've been trying to find more allies to help us fight Mendax. The Veritans faked my death because I was their only hope at saving what was left of Earth. You see, it's more than just oil they're after, Jess. They have much more advanced technology than we do. They mine the resources of all the planets they encounter. But what they really want is the people —the manpower. Mendaxians make promises and then suck a planet dry for years until there's nothing left to give. They use the resources as bargaining power to swindle more planets. When they control the resources, they are able to control more planets. They are able to control more people. Once they fully enslave us, they will move more Mendaxians here. Just as they promised us a place of refuge, they've promised other planets oil, power, water . . ." She rubbed my arm, and the embers of the fire crackled.

She added another log.

The more planets Mendax could collect, the more power they would hold across the galaxies. Their plan was to take over the universe. We were just one small stepping stone in the process. If Mom hadn't stumbled upon the Veritans, we would have never known about the Mendaxians' tactics. The more planets we could contact across other galaxies, the better chance we would have at fighting off these conquistadors of space.

"So, what do we do now?" I asked, still taking in all the information.

"I've spent the last twenty years attempting to recruit other planets to fight with us. Most are too scared, and the other half don't believe me. They think we're the bad guys." She shook her head in frustration. "I've been back and forth throughout the years checking on you. The CIA is used to seeing the Mendaxians in their airspace, but the Mendaxians noticed Veritans were visiting too. They found out I was still alive and sent agents to watch you. They knew how they would find me. But maybe we can use this situation to our advantage. We have Gabe now, and we need to convince them that this is not a good plan. We have to stand up to them." Her demeanor changed, her voice hardening with protection.

"You know Angie is an alien, right?" I asked, feeling a little dumb. But I smiled because of how bizarre the conversation was. Mom had been playing chess this whole time while I was playing checkers.

"Who do you think sent her?" Mom winked, the wrinkles in her forehead coming uncreased.

"So, the five of us have to save the world?" My lungs filled and stretched uncomfortably. Saying it out loud made it scarier.

"Pretty much." The dimple in her face held promise. Her worried smirk matched exactly how I felt inside. We were just trying to doggy paddle our way through this. We didn't really have a choice. Swim or die.

Well, you always said you wanted to be part of something bigger, didn't you?

I guess I thought I would be improving patients' quality of life, one spine at a time. I should have specified what I meant by bigger.

CHAPTER

TWENTY-FIVE

After an hour or so, Dad brought more frozen babies into the shop. I looked down most of the night, passing the time with the animals and avoiding everyone around me. Snow crystals melted off their fuzzy ears. Each time the water evaporated on the concrete floor, Dad walked in with another baby calf. I caught glimpses of myself in my phone reflection. The bags under my eyes bulged and my cheeks were still marked by red blotches. It was like a really fucked-up family reunion. Everyone loved me, but the chaos that they brought to my life didn't feel like love. It kind of felt like torture.

There was a silent agreement not to make any more plans until the morning. We had been hit by so much information; it was safe to say everyone was brain-dead. The world was ending, my crush was a CIA agent, my mom was alive . . . And don't forget that Dad had just found out my best friend was an alien. As we made our way to the house, Gabe followed all of us like a lost puppy dog. He'd quickly gone from badass agent to the bottom of the food chain. Angie held an invisible leash, making sure he didn't stray too far. He was now the only leverage we had to try and convince his colleagues that Mendax did not have good intentions.

Dad was on cloud nine. In fact, while I was in turmoil, the grin on his face didn't falter once. The muscles in his cheeks must have hurt from the joy he felt seeing both of his favorite people in the same room. He stood in the doorway, holding the screen door open for everyone to enter. His mood was contagious, and I couldn't help smiling back. The only problem was, my eyes still sagged with worry. His large hand squeezed my tricep in a gesture of silent comfort before he let the screen door slam behind us.

Angie spoke in low tones, Gabe grunting in response. I had locked myself in the bathroom. I avoided eye contact with the mirror and braced myself against the porcelain pedestal sink. It would take only one more catastrophic life change to watch it shatter beneath the weight of my anger. I lifted my weight off it before that could happen. Cold well water splashed my face as I attempted to wash some of the stress away. I was swishing alkaline minerals and toothpaste around my mouth when I saw a shadow underneath the door.

"Just give me a minute, I'm almost done," I shouted. The heavy wooden door stuck on the old carpet. Before I could step out of the bathroom, Gabe pushed me back inside. He used his body to block the door and raised his arms in surrender.

"I already talked to Ang. Can I just get five minutes?" Gabe pleaded, slowly lowering his hands. He took my silence as permission to continue.

"I just wanted to check in and see how you were feeling. I know this has been a lot, and for the record it has for me too. This was supposed to be an easy—" He cut off mid-sentence.

"Easy what?" I barked.

"They told me it would just be a babysitting gig. I was just supposed to watch you, do my job, and look for the next promotion. It sounds like they kept me in the dark on purpose." His head was down, and he looked up at me from under his thick eyebrows. I didn't have anything left to give, so I shrugged my shoulders.

"I also didn't mean to catch feelings for you. I used my job as an excuse to keep lying to myself. And, well, here we are." He finished and shrugged his own shoulders. My blood curdled into cottage cheese, and I could feel it blocking my arteries and the blood flow to my brain. Gabe was a constant mind game. The parts he played in life were positions of power, knowledge, and leadership. But when he spoke to me, I saw another version. His mask came off for a few moments and he was just Gabe.

He pursed his lips to the side, waiting patiently for me to clear the cottage cheese from my blood. The sharp angles of his face seemed to morph into softer edges. His eyes welcomed my emotions instead of piercing through me. His change in demeanor thinned my blood enough for me to focus on the conversation.

It was so frustrating to be on a roller coaster of emotions with him. My love for him was tainted by anger. The fear of letting him in trumped everything else. But I imagined being friends with me was similar. I was constantly pretending to be someone else.

Maybe we were meant for each other.

"Aren't you the least bit afraid of what will happen to you now? We're literally going to use you as a pawn to get the government to listen and save the world from the bad evil aliens by working with the good hero aliens." I huffed. I decided to collapse onto the toilet. The voice that escaped me was proof that there were still traces of anger and anxiety in my body. The stress of the day and the love frustration didn't mix well.

"I don't know if I can move forward in my position if they continue to make moves with the Mendaxians. I just can't stand for the possibility that this earth could cease to exist if we don't do something," he pleaded.

"What makes you different from the rest of them? How do I know you aren't going to turn around and lie to me again?" I snapped, finding more fire in the pit of my stomach.

"Because I'm your friend, and because regardless of how Angie and I came into your life, we were both sent to protect you. That part hasn't changed. You can choose to hate me, but I was blindsided just as much as you were. I didn't ask for this." He leaned against the closed door, waiting for me to unclench my jaw and relax my eyebrows. I stood up from the toilet and tried to ignore the way my sock felt after stepping in some water on the floor. The cotton squished into my toes right as I was winding up my next comeback. Gabe met me at the sink, and I hardened my stance. I lifted my finger to point it in his face, but he grabbed it before it could get past my waist.

"I won't lie to you again," he said through his teeth. My skin slipped back and forth in the tight grasp of his fingers. My carpals squished together, and I pushed against him.

"Let. Go," I said under my breath. He grabbed my other arm and pulled me closer.

"I promise." His eyes softened even more, and I saw a glimpse of the Gabe I'd met a few years ago. He was younger, meeker. His face lowered closer to mine, and I could feel the tiny bones in my wrist about to crumble. My blood thinned, rushing too quickly to my heart. The liquid was audible, sloshing through each valve faster than the muscle could keep up. Once again, my anger felt like attraction. I tightened my fists, ready to knee him right between the legs. Just as quickly as he had grabbed my arm, he let go and headed out of the bathroom.

"Wait," I said quietly, halfway hoping he wouldn't hear. But when he turned around, I found myself back in the laundry room of that college house. This time I didn't have a drink in my hand, and this time my lips weren't tinged with vodka and Redbull. This time, we didn't stumble.

I found myself back in class, ignoring the way he looked at me, bullying him until he stopped. This time, I didn't ignore him.

I found myself back on the dance floor, his hands around my waist, looking for my next move to use him for my own personal gain. This time, I wasn't looking for my next move.

This time, our faces smashed into each other. Anger, frustration, rage, and tension collided. We fought to open our mouths, knowing that if we broke away from the kiss, we would never let it continue. To assure me he wasn't going anywhere, Gabe grabbed my waist, signaling me to release. With an inhale, I parted my lips and realized I did love him. I always had. I could taste some of the salt from my rehydrated tears, and it fueled my emotions even more. The kiss deepened and he mistook that emotion for desire. His hand began to slip underneath my shirt, and the guillotine sliced the kiss in half.

"I don't trust you that much," I said with my arms wrapped around his neck. I moved my hand to his cheek. "If you lie to me again, I will personally sic Angie on you—the new and improved alien badass Angie." He broke away from me and I tried to avoid eye contact. Sweat seemed to be forming around my hairline. I imagined myself like a dog panting in the hot summer. I shut my mouth, making my breathing even louder through my stuffy nose. Between the crying and the sexual tension, I was a mess.

"Speaking of the boss, she insisted I sleep upstairs with her tonight until we figure out how to move forward with our plan to meet with the higher-ups. I'm guessing the idea won't be well received." His voice seemed to have changed back to the person I knew before I'd uncovered his real identity. A smirk took over his face when he noticed I was still lingering against his body.

"I guess I'd better get some rest anyway. Tonight has been, well . . ." I searched for the words to describe how it felt to meet your long-lost mother and kiss your CIA-agent crush all in the same day. "A lot," I finished.

At the stairs, we went our separate ways. I couldn't help but think somewhere in this chaos, things seemed to finally be feeling normal again. Maybe the problem was that I was meant to be a part of this chaos. My entire life before this was protecting me from it.

CHAPTER
TWENTY-SIX

Silverware clanged and Dad shuffled around the kitchen making breakfast with the limited provisions he had. Five of the six chairs were filled, and it was the liveliest the house had been even before Mom left. I could tell the company overwhelmed and excited him as he fumbled with the pans on the stove. He kept a resealable bag of pancake mix in the pantry.

There was warmth in the room but also some awkwardness. Throats cleared and everyone found something to fiddle with on the table rather than talking to each other.

"Alright, can we just stop acting like we're all nervous around each other? The four of you weren't nervous last night when you were sucking each other's faces," Angie blurted out, taking a sip of her water. Everyone stopped fidgeting and looked down into their laps, embarrassed like children.

"I'm not judging anyone. If I got to see my boyfriend I'd do the same thing. I would actually be doing more than just sucking face!" She smirked, and my face felt as hot as the cast iron that was warming on the stove. Mom started to giggle and eventually everyone relaxed their shoulders.

"I didn't know you had a boyfriend. Like a Veritan boyfriend? Human? You and Harold? Is that a thing?" I stammered, not sure whether other life-forms intermingled in the human world.

"I don't mind humans, but they're lacking in some areas, if you know what I mean." She raised her eyebrows and nodded at Mom and me, waiting for a response.

"So it's a long-distance kind of thing?" I thought of all the nights she'd been on the phone when she told me it was her mom.

"Yeah, it's more like a phone sex kind of thing. I don't know, I'm keeping my options open since both of our worlds may be ending soon." She shrugged her shoulders in response.

Getting to see the new Angie merge with the one I knew was strange. All of her reservations had started to make sense, but it didn't change her personality. She was definitely still her, just from another planet. She wore her human suit, not willing to risk anyone seeing her. The costume was good—really good—but now that I looked closer, I could see what it had been hiding for so long. Her contacts were what made her brown eyes so warm, with the glow of the fluorescence behind them. Her small, athletic build was disproportionate, and her skin oddly too clear. No pores, no blemishes. The silicone suit was easily distinguishable now that I actually looked at her. My faith in humanity plummeted thinking about how she walked amongst us unnoticed, our own kind too wrapped up in themselves to tell.

Gabe looked relieved when Dad set down the pancakes and bacon. He quickly started shoveling food into his mouth to avoid the conversation that Angie was ready to dive deeper into. Luckily for him, Mom had business to discuss, and I wasn't quite sure which conversation was more uncomfortable. I felt like the topic of alien sex was way more interesting and much less stressful.

"Before we can do anything, I'm going to need time. Agents and the Mendaxians have had eyes on me since I left, and I barely got here by the skin of my teeth. We're going to need backup. Bigger ships too. I don't want this to go south, but I have a feeling it will." Mom looked straight at me. When she furrowed her brow, it looked freakishly similar to my reflection in the mirror.

"I've tried to get ahold of the commander, but my signals keep getting intercepted. Ever since the CIA told Jess and Chuck the truth, they've really cracked down on things," Angie added. I took everything in. I was the outsider in this situation. Although I had started to feel a little more at ease, it did frustrate me that I wasn't in control. I felt like a helpless child watching all the adults make the important decisions.

"Before I left, we got word that Mendax is having an Earthside meeting in a few months. They're looking to start pulling oil from the eastern side of the state, hitting all of the rural areas first." Mom brought her gaze to Dad as she finished her sentence.

"They can't do that," he snapped. His lip lifted his mustache into a curtain over his teeth. My dad didn't often show a lot of emotion, but when he did, it frightened everyone. The softness that characterized his face had dissipated. They were after his way of life.

"They'll start with public land first. Then they'll swindle all the country folk into fake deals." She answered his frustration with reasonable facts. We all knew that dollar signs would change anyone's mind. All they had to do was promise money and all our neighbors would take the deal. Farming and ranching wasn't something people did for the money. It was something they did for peace. It was a way to raise families in a smaller area and avoid the noise of the city. But they would offer more money than any of us had ever seen, and the bribe would work. We'd be caught in the Mendaxians' trap.

Dad stewed in the background as the conversation continued. Mom and Angie spoke of our lack of numbers. Veritan was a small planet, but they had one thing that was holding off an attack: a force field engineered to surround their atmosphere. It worked as a repellent, bouncing any intruder off when they tried to enter. Mendaxians used brute force and ignorance to take what they wanted, but Veritans used their brains. The force field could hold off a few ships at a time, but when Mendax was tired of waiting, they would send a fleet to break the barrier. It was only a matter of time.

My attention was set on Mom and Angie's conversation. All the terms and locations were difficult to keep up with, and I noticed myself shifting into a blank state as I tried to decipher them. I could still feel the pain in my wrists, the water on my socks, and the pressure from Gabe's lips. There were so many instances where this moment could have happened. Why did it happen last night?

"What if we're going about this all wrong?" I asked, interrupting the game planning session. Everyone at the round table locked eyes with me at once. The comforting buzz changed to a pressured silence. "Why don't we just have Angie tell them what's going on?"

"Good luck with that." Gabe looked up from his plate.

"You guys said that the Veritans didn't even know Earth existed. The only reason they put up a fight was because they saw neighboring planets being conquered. They're using the distance between galaxies and other planets to their advantage. We just have to prove to them that Mendax is the problem. I mean, come on! Don't you have contact with any other planets since you've been searching for help? There must be some out there that are in way too deep with the Mendaxians. We have to show the CIA what will happen if we take the deal," I added.

Another uncomfortable silence danced around the middle of the table. Everyone was mesmerized by it, pondering the idea I'd just come up with. It was crazy, but maybe just crazy enough.

All at once, the four of them stared up at me.

Mom spoke first. "I wish I had a better idea. But I don't." I could see her fingers tapping against her thumb.

One, two, three, four . . . One, two, three, four . . . She does it too.

"Alright, well that means your job is to get us a date and time for that meeting with Mendax. We have to convince your buddies that we're the good guys before they sell all your souls to the Mendaxian slave trade," Angie directed Gabe. She pointed her tiny finger at him, the wide tips of her fingers holding him there across the room. He finally nodded so she would release her gaze.

"I'll call them and check in. They were expecting me to be here by now, and I can assure them the package has been delivered safely." Gabe's voice did that thing again where it switched from nerdy med student to Agent Harris. "If headquarters thought something was up, we would know by now," he added in a more serious tone. He pushed himself away from the table and held out his hand for his cell phone.

"Easy there, killer. Just because you're in her good graces doesn't mean you're in mine yet. There will be no phone calls without my supervision," Ang commanded before tearing off a piece of chewy bacon with her teeth.

"Alright, alright. I guess I'll just be useless around here and try to blend in while we—" Before Gabe could finish, he was interrupted.

"We're going to need to work on that if you want to blend

in," Dad huffed before taking a swig of coffee. The steam rolled in front of his face. His mustache revealed a small smile, and he looked up at Gabe with a teasing expression, waiting for him to disagree.

"I'll be fine," Gabe answered shortly. He was still pouting about Angie's orders, and now he was getting it from Dad. Even after last night's events, a small part of me still liked seeing him struggle.

"I'm not saying you're not a hard worker, Agent Harris. I'm just saying that if the folks around here see you dressed that way, with your hair all fancy and your lumberjack clothes . . ." Dad looked him up and down, clearly trying his hardest not to cringe. Gabe was beautiful. And it wasn't that it was a bad thing or that there was no one attractive where I came from. It was a lifestyle that was worn on your sleeve. It wasn't just Gabe's outfit. He carried himself like a trained professional. He stood up just a little too straight. His hands weren't calloused from outdoor labor, and his skin wasn't leathered from the sun. He may as well have been an alien too.

"Like what?" Gabe asked, frustrated.

"You look like a freakin' poser, bud. They're going to know something's up immediately." Dad shrugged his shoulders as apology for his bluntness. Everyone at the table started giggling and for the first time in a long time, I didn't feel like I had to fake my emotions. I felt oddly comfortable in the room full of misfits.

Mom and Angie were going to get in touch with the rest of the Veritans. They were trying to use the planet's past experiences to prove to the US that this deal wasn't going to end well. Maybe if they saw proof—pictures, stories from other life-forms—they would change their mind. This wasn't just about a single CIA agent trying to move up the ranks. Entire other planets had suffered the wrath of Mendax. This would need to be executed delicately. We needed backup, but not too much backup. We needed command staff, but not too many soldiers. We wanted to be prepared, but we didn't want to threaten the government. The more attention we brought to the situation, the more likely that the Mendaxians would intervene.

This would be an attempt at a peaceful hostage maneuver. Gabe was our bait, and we had to hope and pray they actually cared about his life. He was the only leverage we had other than heavy weaponry. He was the only way we could possibly get them to listen to Angie. Risking his position in the CIA could save us all.

Until we got Angie in a room with the CIA, we would need to turn Gabe into a cowboy. Mom and Ang would lie low in the house, communicating as much as they could with our off-Earth contacts. Spring brought new babies, which meant double the work on the ranch. We'd have to finish calving and start branding season. Cattle would need moved to new pastures, and help would need traded between other ranches.

We were officially cowboys and aliens.

CHAPTER
TWENTY-SEVEN

"Yeah. Well . . . Mm-hmm. That's great." Dad was on the phone. He kept grunting, trying to interrupt. The awkwardness and the anger contorted every wrinkle on his face. We were crammed in the single cab pickup checking cattle. Angie craned her neck as far as she could to get closer to Dad's ear. Gabe and I shared the other half of the cab. The deep voice on the other end of the line boomed a muffled string of words, confusing the rest of us. Dad shook his head at us in disappointment, patiently waiting for the other person to end the call. Angie started tapping on her mobile device, communicating with Mom back at home. Mom wasn't exactly on the best terms with the United States, so she couldn't risk being seen out and about. Not to mention that everyone else still thought she was dead.

After we'd decided how to move forward with the Mendaxians, work proceeded on the ranch. We had set up a communications center upstairs, and Gabe was in cowboy bootcamp. Things seemed to be going well, but the look on Dad's face concerned me. The rambling continued as the pickup followed along the deep two-tracks that had been carved over time.

I tapped my toe uncontrollably. My ears tried to decipher the information that was coming through the other side of the phone, but the rest of my body yearned to be closer to Gabe.

"Hey." A low whisper distracted my ears for a split second. Gabe steadied my tapping leg with his hand, squeezing tight around my thigh. "We're OK."

The garbled cell phone conversation fell by the wayside. I threaded my arm through his and leaned closer. His slower heart rate acted as an anchor, digging deep to the ocean floor to slow the rhythm of my own body.

"Damnit!" Angie shouted. We both retracted our arms to our respective spaces in the cab.

"They're already making deals with our neighbors. I thought this wasn't supposed to happen until after the meeting?" Dad slammed his palms against the steering wheel. Our spines straightened in unison. "I didn't know what to say. How do you tell someone to turn down a five-million-dollar contract?" The disappointment pulled his shoulders forward, and his eyes seemed to look into our future for the first time. It hadn't been real for him until now.

"We have brandings coming up. The most social time of the year for all of us," I said, addressing the weary feeling in the cab. "No one knows how Gabe and I met. Let's fake a relationship and tell everyone he's a lawyer." My words came out panicked, but each new obstacle that was set before us seemed to be an opportunity for me to help.

"A fake relationship?" Angie huffed under her breath. She was right. That part was laughable, but the rest wasn't. In fact, I'd surprised even myself with the ideas I had come up with lately. I was just as good at making shit up as the rest of them.

"We just have to tell them we got the same deal and ask to

look over the paperwork with them. Convince them that this is a trick." I ignored Angie. Dad and Gabe nodded in unison.

"It could work." Gabe smiled and bumped me with his shoulder, forcing my body into Angie and hers into Dad.

"It could. But we still don't know what to tell the CIA." Angie looked serious.

"I can get us a meeting, but we're depending on you to convince them," Gabe answered her.

The heater blared, white noise to fill the stale air. We had no ideas yet. It was Mendax's word against ours.

"I have an idea. It's risky, but it could work." The spark in Angie's eyes dimmed. Her snarky character smoldered as a cold front of emotions seemed to shudder through her body. We waited for the plan, but nothing came out of her already open mouth.

"Ang, you there?" I prodded.

"I have a brother," she said.

"And?" Now I was being snarky.

"He's half Mendaxian," Angie said blankly. Gears started turning, squeaking and groaning with the new knowledge she'd presented. My brain worked overtime trying to accommodate another piece of the disastrous puzzle we were trying to solve. My mind had spoken a thousand words, but my mouth sat open, much like the rest of the pickup.

"But, how?" Gabe finally broke the pregnant pause, asking the question we all wanted the answer to.

"The commander that we've all been talking about. That's my mom." She waited a while for the rest of us to follow the story she was about to tell. Her position to protect me seemed even more fitting. We were both the daughters of leaders, unknowingly playing a huge part in this intergalactic war of resources. "She was sent on a mission with the previous commander to broker peace between the two planets. They were both captured, tortured, and raped. They pressed for information on how to destroy the shield around our planet. They didn't budge. By the time backup arrived, the commander was dead. They saved Mom, but she unknowingly carried a Mendaxian child—Luke." She trailed off.

"Then she became the new commander?" Gabe ignored the emotional sensitivity of the moment, and suddenly I was repulsed by his body leaning so closely against mine.

"Where's your brother now?" I asked, more concerned.

"No one accepted him on Veritan. As the son of a leading military commander, he was an embarrassment. How would someone who looked like our enemy ever be accepted into our society?" Angie shrugged her shoulders before continuing. My heart hurt as she spoke about someone she clearly loved. "Mom had to hide her feelings, keep leading the fight against the Mendaxians regardless of the way she felt about her son. She was revered for her bravery but criticized for her decision to keep him. So he left—went to Mendax and never came back. She shed a single tear and never spoke of it again." Angie's sentence ended with a slightly higher pitch, iridescent liquid welling up in her brown contacts.

"Do you have contact with him?" Gabe intruded again. Angie fiddled with her bracelet, a thick metal cuff she wore every day. The pearly tears dripped onto dull stones, bringing the bracelet to life. The oxidized metal suddenly brightened to silver, and its black stones turned to teal. The teardrops seemed to swirl in the stones, bringing forth a vibrant glow.

"Mom told me that I wasn't allowed to contact him after he left; it was too dangerous. Luke was my best friend, and her position ripped us apart." Angie's tears stopped falling, but I couldn't take my eyes off the unassuming jewelry that had adorned her wrist for so long. Her eyes caught my curiosity. "He left me this. Said to use it when I needed him. It's never done that before." Angie had just noticed the bracelet transforming, unaware that I'd been staring at it for the last few minutes. The radio screeched strange noises and static loudened inside the cab of the pickup.

Dad pulled over at our destination to break ice. The tank of frozen water was surrounded by parched cattle, but once we opened the doors of our squished clown car Chevy, they scattered.

"Get back! I don't know what's going to happen!" Angie yelled, motioning with her right arm to get away. Her wrist flickered with light, and luminescent swirls created a vortex in the sky above her.

Digital pixels swarmed and a male voice spoke.

"Angela. Angela, can you hear me?" The voice suddenly had a face. Within a few seconds, Luke was in front of us.

TWENTY-EIGHT

A MUSCLED FIGURE TOOK SHAPE AS THE PIXELS ALIGNED AND THE static in his voice started to clear. He was scaled, reptilian. But his facial features resembled Angie's—round eyes with gleaming green irises and a soft button nose that did not match his chiseled cheekbones. His differences made me realize why he'd never been accepted. He looked so similar to his sister, yet so completely different. He was a walking reminder of the enemy at hand. Except he was handsome, and his eyes carried the same kindness that I'd seen in Angie's for years. I continued to scan the image, taking in his crimson scales, finding beauty in the mixture of the Veritan I knew and the Mendax I had never seen.

"Lucious, it's you." Angie exhaled a breath of relief. She looked down at her bracelet, still looking confused by the trinket her brother had left her.

"It's tear activated. I've only ever seen you cry once, and that was when I left. If I had given you my contact, you would have been calling me every day." Luke's white teeth gleamed as he smiled at his sister. His protruding canines startled me, like a cross between vampire and snake. I straightened my body to disguise my shiver of fear. In the short pause, I could hear cows mooing in the background, and I saw everyone else studying the image as closely as I was. "We don't have much time." Luke's voice turned harsh, and all of us flinched.

"Are you safe?" Angie blurted. Luke's eyes darted around him as he made sure no one was listening.

"I'm part of the rebellion. Taking this call is a risk." Loud clanks of metal leaked through the audio. "I'm working in the mines with the Mendaxians and the others enslaved by our leaders here."

"We need you to come here to convince the Earth leaders not to make the same mistake."

"You want me to go to Earth? In this war climate? Sounds like Mom's efforts to stay out of other people's business aren't going so well." A tinge of sarcasm and hate laced his words, and the rest of us looked down. Suddenly we were intruding on a very intimate conversation between siblings.

"If we don't gain allies, we're in the same boat, brother." Angie spoke through a closed mouth, challenging his anger. He rolled his eyes. Their dynamic was full of love and familiarity, reminding me that Angie had become like a sister to me over the years. Luke's protective voice and lecturing tone reminded me of the way she spoke to me.

"And you think they're going to help you?" He gestured around at all of us and suddenly I felt like a useless human. "I knew when Agent Rodriguez started going back to check on her that there would be problems."

How many times had she been back to check on me?

"Can you get here or not?" Angie barked. The softness seemed to return to Luke's face. "The CIA has a meeting in two weeks to start their invasion."

"And you think because I look like them, I can convince them . . ." Suddenly the call made sense for Luke. His glowing eyes stared off. I wondered how he would get here undetected. "Give me five days."

"Perfect," I interjected into the conversation. His eyes met mine, and I watched him grit his teeth. Was he worried? Embarrassment rose to my cheeks. Each time I started to feel more confident in myself, someone with more power and experience popped into the scene to take me down a peg.

"I have one stipulation, though." Luke used his light-filled eyes to strike fear through my soul. He turned and gave Angie the same look. "You can't tell Mom. Or Agent Rodriguez. If I'm going to risk my life to save these humans, then I don't need the almighty Veritan getting in my way."

Damn, that was harsh.

"Deal." Angie spoke before I could argue. The clanking in the background started to get louder.

"Five days," he answered. With a flash, he was gone. It resembled an old TV screen being switched off, the static and pixels sucked back into the bracelet. We all stared aimlessly into the cold, gray sky.

Dad scraped the ax and the pitchfork off of the flatbed and continued the job we'd set out to do. We sat stagnant as he used his work to process the next steps. The cool air cleared my constricted throat, releasing some of the tension I'd been holding throughout the conversation. Gabe spoke with Angie near the truck as I watched Dad complete the job alone.

"Gabe, your cowboy training is moving up a level this Saturday." I spoke facing Dad, realizing he needed to hear this too. Spring bantered with winter, signifying an upcoming change on the ranch. The more consistent warm weather and influx of baby calves meant branding season was upon us. Winter was lonely on the ranch, but it was about to get a lot more social in the days to come. It was a community effort to identify, vaccinate, and care for the newly welcomed calves. It was also a perfect time for me and Gabe to use the gatherings as a weapon against the CIA and Mendaxian offers. There was power in numbers, and it was our job to convince the other ranchers that there were no good deals to be made with the government.

"Do I get to ride a horse?" Gabe asked, giddy with excitement.

I had spoken with several of our neighbors about trading help. So far, all they knew was that I was home for a few months and that Dad had new day help. Gabe grabbed the pitchfork from Dad, launching the large pieces of ice into the dirt beside him. Mama cows brought their babies over the hill again, inspecting to see if the coast was clear.

Gabe's hips twisted as he pitched more and more ice into the dirt around an impatient crowd of cows. Their eyes followed each stroke of his pitchfork, and mine found the tapering of the hand-me-down jeans we'd found him in Dad's closet. The worn cotton creased where his glutes and quads met, accentuating parts of him I wanted to ignore. Admittedly, his efforts on the ranch had been noticeable. He'd pulled calves from womb to soil. He'd helped chase a few back to their respective pastures on foot. But the daily chores, the feeding and watering, those weren't hard to catch on to. I needed him to fit in—be accepted. We needed our neighbors to listen.

"Why do you think you need to ride?" Dad gave a stern look as he loaded the ax back onto the pickup.

"Well, if I'm going to go help these other ranchers, shouldn't I learn to do all the cool stuff that you do? You know, like roping, chasing cows . . . that kind of thing?" Gabe looked around at all of us, waiting for us to defend him against Dad.

"Come on, I've been doing just fine." His excitement was childlike.

"You're not ready." I blew out the flame that was igniting his irises. His mouth drooped when I didn't smile.

"You'll be ground crew," Dad added.

"Ground crew?" Gabe looked defeated.

"You're the bottom of the totem pole here. You don't get to rope and do all of the fun stuff until you've put in your time. Don't worry, we'll get you on a horse before all of this is over," Dad said, attempting to reassure him. I focused on the last part of his sentence. When what was over? The world? The ranch? Gabe's job that included "protecting" me?

"You have to fit in," I said, ending the conversation before we all packed ourselves into the pickup to drive home.

Sometimes when the brain is bleeding, there's too much pressure inside the skull. I suddenly related to the patient that I'd once assisted with during my clinicals, when I'd drilled a hole in her head to relieve that pressure. Except there was no one here to drill a hole in my skull. The pressure from a triangular relationship between planets in different galaxies was about to implode what little working brain matter I had left.

I was in love with Gabe. He was a known liar.

We had leverage against Mendax. But, again, we had to lie in order to use it.

Our friends trusted us. And we'd also have to pull the wool over their eyes to save their lives. The moving parts of the situation created so much chaos in the grooves of squishy brain tissue. I touched my ear. To my surprise, there was nothing leaking from the orifices of my head. But my face must have been twisted as I tried to endure the deluge of thoughts that consumed me.

"This is my job. I made you like me, after all," Gabe let out a low whisper. Unfortunately, he was right. It reassured me and bothered me at the same time.

"This isn't the same. Cowboys are ruthless." My voice was loud enough for the rest to hear. I looked to Dad for reassurance. Instead, he rolled his eyes, denying the truth. That eye roll—the attitude and the judgment—was exactly what scared me. The others would act the same.

"Remember that acting class we took in undergrad?" Angie blurted out.

"What does that have to do with anything?" Gabe's face puckered in annoyance and confusion. It was one of those looks that made me reconsider my attraction to him.

"Yes, the improv exercise!" She turned to me and Gabe, waiting for us to remember. She huffed when we didn't reply. "You have to accept any and all information. We're going to be acting, so if anyone says something that seems off, don't question it." Angie cast a long stare in my direction. The advice was for me. Although I was good at masking my emotions on the daily, I had a hard time not taking things literally. If we got caught in a situation where someone had to make something up, I was the weak link.

"Well, neither of you should have a problem with that since you've been doing it my entire adult life." I narrowed my eyes in response to her concerned look. Dad slowed the pickup as we approached the house. Angie and Gabe continued to stare. "Alright. I got it. Don't question it. Just go with it."

"Chuck, how do you feel about keeping this on the downlow? Can you lie to your wife?" Angie added.

"If it means I get to spend more time with her, then yes," he replied with gusto. It made me sad to realize how long he had spent alone without the company of his one true love. It was even sadder that he knew their reunion probably wouldn't last much longer.

Mom was waiting for us inside, and the little secret tickled the nerves attached to my stomach lining. This time, I was a liar. But for now, I was going to call it acting.

Don't question it. Just go with it.

CHAPTER
TWENTY-NINE

Our presence usually awoke the old ranch house, making the floors creak and the furnace yawn as it shivered from the cold air let through its doors. But when we entered with those secrets, it knew. Our breath seemed to rasp against our windpipes, and our boots seemed to crash against the concrete as if they had been dropped from skyscraper buildings. Our warm and humble home knew what was upon us. And the ease I'd felt since being home was suddenly gone.

As I untied my left boot, I met Angie's eyes. They pierced through me like I was a small child who was being warned in front of a crowd of people. Her concern was valid, but it still annoyed me that she thought I would put our lives in jeopardy.

"Come with me, I want to show you something." She pranced through the quiet kitchen, passed the living room, and made her way upstairs where Mom kept her communications center. Computer screens lit up the dark attic-like room I used to sleep in. The closets where the eyes used to watch me were wide open, and the curtain to the window on the front of the house was closed. Mom didn't pause to look up when we entered the room.

"We have a meeting set up in five days with the CIA. They'll be coming out here to check on things and look at a few concerns that Gabe had. We aren't telling them any more details." Angie's words unglued Mom's eyes from the screen.

"And? What are you going to tell them?" Mom said, snapping a little.

"I'm going to tell them about my brother." Angie's tone ended in a question, but I knew she intended for it to be a statement. She was acting—acting unsure, acting like she hadn't already made plans to have him come speak with the CIA. The statement masquerading as a question was enough to make Mom spin her chair and shove it behind her as she stood up.

"Are you insane? Who's to say they don't already know about him? A mixed-race being banished from the planet they already don't trust." She rose taller than either of us. I trained my eyes on the tilted ceiling, concerned she would smack her head if she rose any taller. "Sounds like a great idea. Mendax-ians are flooding our airspace right now, and the last thing we need is to make Veritan look worse than it already does."

"We have to show them the preservation of Veritan and what Mendax actually looks like. My brother wasn't banished. He left by choice." Angie stood her ground. "He's sent me pictures of the mines, Rodriguez. He's a Mendaxian slave as we speak."

Acting.

Telling the truth but not the whole truth wasn't a bad idea. It was a way to feel less guilty about lying. She was trying to make things easier for me.

"And how do you know they'll believe you?" Mom kept questioning.

"We have no other choice." Angie put an end to the conversation. Behind them, something on the screen distracted me—a scene with clear blue water, vibrant colors, and plants that looked plastic, waxy, and tropical. Buildings protruded from the water.

"What is that?" My curiosity dampened the fire at hand.

Mom turned to see what had caught my eye. "That's Veritan." People like Angie walked through water cities, making their way through the landscape of the vacation paradise screen saver I thought I was looking at. It looked so peaceful I thought it was fake. But it wasn't. It was a livestream of where Mom had gone into hiding. Fortunately for her, it looked more like a resort. "The planet of truth and water—the reason Mendax wants it so badly."

"Were you saving the world or enjoying an extended vacation?" Now I was the fire that needed putting out. This entire time, it seemed like Mom had been out blasting bad guys and living in an unknown world full of fear. Up until now, I'd only seen distant pictures of the planets and their locations. Small dots indicated the enemies' whereabouts between galaxies. But the picture of where Mom had taken refuge ignited a sense of anger I hadn't felt since she'd come home. I had forgiven her for her absence, but this made resentment sneak back into my soul.

My eyebrows pulled together so hard it felt like the muscles were drawing pain from my entire body and depositing it right behind my eyes. The headache that radiated through my optic nerves brought nausea and discomfort, antagonizing my anger. Mom looked at Angie, Angie looked at me, and I closed my eyes, looking for relief. When I opened them, Angie was heading down the stairs. She paused at the banister before completely exiting the room.

"I think I'll just give you guys some space." She sounded

uneasy, her hand lingering on the iron railing that kept her from falling over the edge of the stairs.

I got the impression that she wanted to rip the banister off the studs in the floor, but she finally let go.

"We haven't really had a chance to talk." Mom's voice pulled my eyes from the twisted iron. She sat and spun her chair, directing her body at me. Her hands gripped her knees in anticipation. I crossed my arms in front of me, mirroring her body language. I couldn't look at her; the frog that had recently taken up permanent residence in my throat seemed to have spawned a million croaking babies. The bigger they got and the more emotions that this whole alien catastrophe caused, the harder it was to hold in my tears.

"I don't know what to say." I finally looked up, locking eyes with her. "Who are you?" Uncrossing my arms seemed to allow her to relax her shoulders. I wanted the truth, but at the same time I didn't. The more secrets she had, the easier it felt to keep this small secret from her.

"I was part of the CIA before you were born, before I even met your dad. Not many people know of the division that works with extraterrestrials, and I'm one of the reasons. If people knew the truth, they would never stand for it. We're one of the only planets that has depleted our resources as fast as we have." She trailed off, realizing she was only talking business again. It was easy to talk about work, but she had pushed her family away to ease the pain. We were similar in that sense.

"Yeah, I get that. But why not take us with you? Why not let Dad know what was going on? You couldn't trust your own family?" The frogs in my throat boiled in my anger, and when I swallowed, I saw her chest tighten with a breath, building up the wall between us again. "Mom, you abandoned us."

"It isn't that simple, Jessica," she said bluntly.

"Sometimes I feel like I would have rather lived a life with my mom and had the world end a little early than live a lie." I might as well have had a noose around her neck. Air was getting harder for her to grasp as I let out the pent-up feelings I'd been suppressing my entire life.

"I know, and I'm sorry. I'm so sorry, but either way, they would have tried to kill me. I knew, and the memory wiping didn't work. It was safer to fake my death and lead them away from the Veritans than put you in danger. I just wanted you to be safe." Tears welled in her eyes, and I started to get up from my chair.

"We can't change it." I clenched my fists as I spat out my reply. She grabbed my arm. It was like when Gabe had held me in the bathroom. I wanted to flee, and these people never let me. They never let me run. I was good at running, but they wanted me to feel safe. Their touch felt uncomfortable, but the security was something I had yearned for. There was finally someone there holding me, grounding me.

"I'm here now, though. I'm here. Now." Mom found my other arm and brought me back around to face her. I gave in and plopped back into the office chair. I pulled away, searching for the loose fabric on the upholstery, grasping at anything that would bring the boiling water in my throat down to room temp.

"You know what the worst part is? I can't stop feeling like the last twenty years of my life were all for nothing." She waited patiently as I pulled small threads out of the chair. I grabbed each one and let it float to the ground, focusing on each fiber rocking back and forth until it hit the floor. "Everything I did was . . . It was out of spite. I hated you. I wanted to make Dad proud. All I did was burn myself to the ground." I rubbed a clump of fibers together with my thumb and pointer finger and let go when I was ready to be done talking.

For years, I'd searched for who I wanted to be, pushing myself to exhaustion, repressing the person I really was. And even though she spoke of her remorse, there was more to the story. But for right now, I didn't care. Because I was hiding something too.

"Everything you did has led you to where you are now. And who you are is exactly what the world needs. We need someone to be brave. We have to save the world, Jess." She met my gaze through the floating thread. Her eyebrows lifted, revealing her wet lashes and water-filled wrinkles. "I can't take it back, and I can't change the past. But I want you to know I saw you. I watched you this whole time. I am so proud of you." She finished her sentence and locked the computer screens.

The few frogs that had survived my anger leapt at the last phrase. They let out one single tear, and I stood up once more. This time Mom didn't grab me. She watched as I got closer to her, and this time I wrapped my long arms around her, her small frame melting against mine.

"I'm proud of you too, Mom."

The secrets were for protection, and although they hurt, they were necessary.

In five days, our secret would either save the world or end it.

CHAPTER
THIRTY

ONLY FOUR DAYS LEFT.

The more I thought about it, my life was full of secrets. People knew only the parts of me that I had specially constructed. There were parts of me I hid to protect myself, and others I hid to make people feel more comfortable. The secrets of the world kept the public safe. Everyone else was able to live their lives normally while forces above them worked to destroy them. Ignorance was bliss. Secrets were absolutely necessary. I thought of how much easier it would have been if med school was my only worry.

I was so naïve.

Pickups and trailers clogged the only entryway leading to our neighbor's house. One by one we made our way down the dirt road and parked in the open area near their barn. The engine went dead, and so did my head. The dirt that still clouded the road dissipated and went straight to my lungs. Today's interactions were crucial. It was the perfect chance for Gabe to practice his cowboy skills, and our opportunity to talk government corruption with the neighbors.

Greetings began as soon as we parked, and the new intro-
ductions were something I would have to lead in Dad's
absence. The trailers bounced as we unloaded heavy saddled
animals onto the dirt. They were ready to gather the new
spring babies. Gabe watched in awe, and I nudged him a few
times to remind him to close his mouth. A little boy's dream to
see real life cowboys never seemed to die, and even though he
was moving up the ranks of the CIA, he hadn't put his time in
here. He was like fresh meat to a pack of wolves.

"You must be the new day help over at the Grays' place." A
large, burly man threw his right hand out to Gabe. The pearl
snaps on his shirt were about to pop from the weight of his
belly, and my eyes darted back to Gabe. I was praying the
buttons didn't explode and hit me right in the eye. "My name
is Trip Grinstead. I neighbor you to the east." Gabe flinched,
shaking Trip's hand and nodding. He looked to me to do the
talking.

"This is Gabe. He's going to be working with us over the
summer to help me and Dad. The operation has grown in the
last few years. Old man bit off more than he can chew." I
instinctively put my hand on Gabe's arm, slapping it with a
little more force than necessary.

I was becoming my father.

A tight smile formed on my face, giving the impression that
I was a proud parent to Gabe. Trip didn't notice the awkwardness, but I could feel my invisible facepalm on my forehead.
Dad had always been the head honcho, and I still felt like the
little girl grabbing at his pant leg.

Before I knew it, cowboys and cowgirls swarmed us, their
spurs clinking all around. I imagined Gabe's limb falling off
from how hard it was being grasped and shook. The tendons in
his arm flexed at the exaggerated grip as he tried to assert his
dominance.

Men.

In unison, Gabe's new friends mounted their horses. As their hooves transitioned from the grass to the county road, the clippity clops got quieter.

"You nervous?" I asked Gabe when most of the horses had disappeared over the hill.

"I think you're more nervous than I am." Gabe looked down at me, then to my hands. *One, two, three, four. One, two, three, four.* I pressed down with my thumbnails, grounding myself in the pressure against my callouses.

"I'm fine." I dusted pretend dirt off my jeans as Gabe's eyes returned to my face. "I'm not used to doing all the talking, the socializing, politicking," I answered with a little bit more ease. Getting that out in the open relaxed me. I was also nervous about talking about the real issue at hand. How many ranches had been hit by these killer oil deals?

"I've seen you in some high-pressure situations when we were doing our clinicals, and that never made you as nervous as all of this." He nudged me with his whole body. While I was distracted, a dirt clod tripped me up and I stumbled, crashing into the side of the neighbors' metal barn. I gave into the fall, sliding down the slick surface. Before my ass hit the dirt, Gabe grabbed my hand, coaxing me up to his level.

"Yeah, well, I've seen you in many types of situations and you never looked as much like a giddy schoolgirl as you do now." I diverted the focus to him, except he had me trapped against the barn. He rolled his eyes, confirming his own embarrassment. I tried to duck underneath the arm that leaned over me.

"You're just jealous. It isn't easy being good at everything. CIA agent, doctor, and now a cowboy . . ." His eyes darkened, and it was no longer his arm that had me trapped. I tried to sneer at him, but he stared at my lips.

"Just follow my lead. Don't try to show off. Flanking calves is all about technique. Just because you're a behemoth of a man doesn't mean you can—"

"Would you just kiss me?" He watched my lips, and I stared at his eyes.

"You cut me off." My closed mouth turned my words into an angry mumble. His long dark lashes swept over his cheek before he looked back up at me.

Long bellows rolled over the hills behind us.

"Follow my lead." I finally ducked under his arm and let out a breath.

I needed to focus.

Over the hill, cowboys made a C shape behind the herd, building a wall made of horses. The amount of bodies made the job move quickly, and before we knew it, the bovines funneled into the large corrals near the barn.

The volume increased. The seductive smile was wiped from Gabe's face as riders sorted a cluster of mama cows off into another pen. The frantic mothers shook the ground as they charged toward the humans looking after their babies.

When I moved forward, Gabe didn't follow.

"Are you coming, tough guy?" The metal gate was cold. I considered whether I should leave him behind. The fear in his eyes was something real. It wasn't fear of death. He was afraid to embarrass himself. The moos became white noise, and I gave him one more look before I swung the gate open.

"I'm coming!" Gabe ran to catch up. He tore the gate from my hand and left me behind to the branding pit. Cowboys were dismounting, the branding irons took to the flame, and red-hot letters were made ready to mark the cattle. There were new faces, younger versions of the men I grew up around. Sons and daughters took their places in the rotation. Gabe found a place beside Trip, gravitating toward someone he'd connected with. That was his way in. He only needed one of them to approve.

The first calf was dragged to the irons, and a stout sorrel mare held the rope tight while two younger kids took the animal to the ground in one swift movement. Gabe scanned the pens and studied the teenagers. A bottle of medicine bubbled as I turned it upside down and plunged the needle of a syringe through the rubber top. The yellow liquid filled the syringe. As I tapped the plastic column to remove the bubbles, I snuck a look across the pen.

He saw me looking through the smoke. Burnt hair tickled my nostrils and I managed a prideful smile. He knew I liked his new look—this rugged vibe he was leaning into.

His Wranglers hugged his shape from the bottom of his belt all the way down to the back of his knees. Trip guided him to a calf coming full speed to the branding irons, and Gabe mimicked the teenagers that had gone before him. Trip grabbed the rope; the calf's back legs were at the mercy of the horse pulling it. As soon as Gabe took the front end of the squirming animal, my nerves melted away. His arms reared back on the leg of the calf as it bucked against him. Gabe steadied the calf with his knee, leaning his weight into its neck.

"Jess, you got the vaccinations?" Trip motioned at me from across the branding pens. The propane that fueled the fire roared, and the moaning of angry mama cows muffled his voice. My arm still held the empty bottles of meds upside down, and I finally snapped out of it.

Gabe leaned over the calf in his white shirt, which reminded me of the one he'd worn at CIA headquarters. The smoke from the burning hair continued to billow over Trip and Gabe as I composed myself.

"Move your knee," I directed without emotion. I turned the needle down, preparing to inject the vaccination into the calf's muscle. My eyes burned and my head was high from the commotion . . . and from Gabe's face. His green eyes, his new facial hair, his lightly tousled hair.

I absolutely hated him.

A yelp sprang from his mouth as I squeezed the trigger on the syringe, and when I looked down, yellow liquid was oozing from his jeans.

"Fuck!" I yelped back, and Trip giggled at me through the cloud that was disappearing from the scene.

"Not the first time someone got poked!" Trip looked down his nose at the blood staining Gabe's jeans. I quickly found the neck of the animal, this time keeping focused on the hairy target instead of Gabe's face. With a quick click, the vaccination found the right animal. My face flushed red, and I hid underneath the ball cap I was wearing.

The folks who were nearby chuckled at Gabe's first battle wound. He smiled and went along with the banter while I slowly sunk into a black hole of embarrassment. I'd been so worried about him fitting in when I was the one stumbling.

Over the next few hours, I tripped four times, got ran over by a runaway calf, and accidentally knocked over a bucket of bloody testicles cut off the bulls as they came through the branding line. Gabe shook hands and made more friends in the flanking lines, and I watched like an idiot on the sidelines.

When the roar of the funneled flame stopped, everyone gathered for beers at the beds of their pickups, waiting for the call to go eat lunch. Trip shoved a beer in my hand before I could fully enter the circle of the branding crew. Cowshit-stained jeans and dirt-covered faces welcomed me, and I realized the only thing that set Gabe apart from the rest was that I was attracted to him. Other than that, he looked like everyone else, like he belonged.

The condensation from the beer dripped into the dirt, and I

pulled the tab, releasing some foam and catching it with my lips. The crowd reminded me of why I used to drink as I took three long gulps from the can. Maybe the alcohol would numb some of the social pain this was causing me.

"So, when are you guys getting married?" a man asked from across the circle. I didn't recognize him from the past, but I knew he was a hired hand for the Gibbons ranch. I almost choked on the fourth gulp of alcoholic fizz. The beer filled my mouth, but there was no place for it to go, and my cheeks bulged at the pressure of the liquid.

"She wants a long engagement. But I wouldn't mind going to the courthouse tomorrow!" Gabe boasted, and Trip slapped his shoulder in approval.

So much shoulder slapping.

"Your dad never said anything about you quittin' the whole doctor thing, Jess. We knew something was up! But from the looks of the way you're suckin' that beer down, it isn't a shotgun wedding." Trip looked down at my stomach. I stopped gulping, taking three small swallows in order to get the rest of the beer down.

"We're just taking a break while we figure out if we're going to move back, right, honey?" Gabe took a swig from the beer he was nursing, toying with me on my home field.

He was getting back at me.

When we got back to the Smiths' house, folding tables full of crockpots, casserole dishes, and large Tupperware lined the garage. The beer in my stomach sloshed like the waves of a tsunami, and the food brought a tingling feeling to my cheeks.

Do not puke.

Gabe was on his third buckskin beer. Trip chuckled, his large hand completely enveloping the can. He looked at me for approval as he handed Gabe the beverage. My tolerance for alcohol really had lowered since I'd come home, and I managed to give a strained smile.

They had accepted him. Now all we had to do was look at those contracts.

The dinner rolls wrapped in a tea towel at the end of the buffet line gave off an aroma of carbs and butter. They were my only hope to get my mind and my body steady. As the heat of the day increased, the pressure of the situation also rose. When the first bite of bread hit the crashing waves in my stomach, I could feel it start to soak up the poison I had been relying on for so long. The meal in front of me started to smell better, and I listened in on Gabe's conversation.

"Yeah, I just finished law school. Trying to figure out what I want to do next." Gabe looked over at me, ready to hand off the baton.

"Think we're both just at a standstill. We're kind of over the big city life," I added, pushing away the sleepy eyes that all those carbs induced.

"Oh, I feel that!" Trip didn't seem to have a quiet volume. His settings included loud and even louder. He walked over to the cooler, grabbing two more beers. Suddenly the bench felt hard and rigid against the bones in my ass as I shifted on the metal picnic table.

This is it.

The bench was like a teeter-totter, and when his large mass plopped down, I was lifted momentarily into the air.

"Speaking of the big city . . . Word around here is they're peddling some pretty good deals for the new oil they found." I raised my eyebrows, and Trip leaned forward to meet my gaze. Gabe sat between us, ready to go in for the kill.

"Can I tell ya something, Jess?" Trip leaned even farther toward Gabe, wrapping his arm around him to get us all closer. Tobacco and beer condensation droplets found their way to my nose. The sudden urge to puke returned. Gabe and I both waited for him to continue. "I got a contract from one of those city slickers. Somethin' ain't right." The cracking of the aluminum seal on his beer can broke the silence, and we all sat up.

"What do you mean?" Gabe played dumb. If we had one person on our side, the rest of the neighboring ranches would follow. I looked around to see if anyone else was listening. Two tables away, the Gibbons ranch hand met my eyes, looking down as if he'd interrupted a conversation. He was young, nervous to be around so many older cowboys. I could relate.

"I worked oil before I came out here. Doesn't work like that. They haven't even surveyed the land and they're out here shakin' money in our faces. Doesn't sit right with me." The foam from the beer collected on his red mustache.

"How about I take a look at the contract?" Gabe slurred his words a little.

Shit, this dude is drunk.

"By God, you're a lawyer, huh? Tell ya what. Why don't you just follow me home and we can give 'er a look together." Trip wasn't fazed by the beers; his body to alcohol ratio was much larger than Gabe's.

Mission accomplished.

THIRTY-ONE

THREE DAYS LEFT.

The picture window revealed Dad graining horses. They followed him like ducks behind their mother in a line that established their own pecking order. One by one, the rubber tubs were filled with sweet grain and the horses enjoyed their treats before they found their way to the barn for saddling.

Since I'd been home, there hadn't been a reason to be in the saddle. But it was time to bring our boots back out from winter hibernation. The last time I wore them I'd barely been able to remove my right boot from my swollen ankle. The last time I wore my riding boots, I was sent hobbling through a pasture to find my horse. They sat in my closet, still covered in the mud that had adhered to them. The leather squeezed the top of my foot when I shoved my heel toward the bottom of my first boot. The stiff material protested against my toes.

Last night after sobering up on our drive to Trip's, we'd examined the faulty contract. There wasn't much that needed done now. The word of mouth from ranch to ranch and farm to farm would travel quickly. The "agency" that had offered deals for the oil rights had included a sneaky clause in the contract. It stated they would be able to take residency if needed, a red flag that was easily missed in the fine print. It didn't seem like a big deal, but occupancy of the entire eastern side of the state would be an easy way to quietly house government agents. Or Mendaxians . . .

I heard Gabe's slow gait coming down the stairs, and I quickly slipped on my second boot.

"What's on the agenda for today?" he questioned, giddier than he should have been. He leaned against my doorway, one arm gripping the top of the doorframe. I needed to figure out what type of clothes he needed, so I used the opportunity to trace his body with my eyes. Before he could enjoy the satisfaction of me checking him out, I focused on his socks.

"Did you bring any boots?" I shifted my gaze back to his eyes. When he stared at the logo on the tip of his toes with confusion, I snuck one more peek at his outstretched arm. We were going to separate all the moms with calves from the rest of the herd. The rest of the girls who hadn't calved yet or who'd lost their babies to the winter would stay behind. We would take them to the sorting pens and put the pairs near the house for processing.

"Now I'm nervous." He raised his eyebrows with worry. I'd found an old pair of Dad's riding boots while I was putting mine on. I dropped them at his feet where he had sat down on the recliner in the living room. So far, he had seen the cowboy life, but he had yet to experience it from the back of a horse. I swam in a sea of my own ego, knowing I would finally be better at something than him. Riding was something that could feel awkward if you didn't grow up doing it. Maintaining your posture, moving with the horse, and looking for the animal's cues can be difficult the older you get. For children it comes naturally. And for most of us that grow up riding, it becomes part of us. Just as you learn to ride a bike, you learn to ride a horse. It always comes back to you.

"Don't worry, Dad will put you on someone old," I reassured him as I opened the door. I looked on the hat rack for an old lid that Dad didn't use anymore. Letting someone wear your hat wasn't necessarily good etiquette, but in this case, I didn't think he would mind. I found a sweat-stained number that was a little too bent up. Gabe had earned his cowboy hat at this point whether I liked it or not.

He leaned forward, waiting to be crowned. I felt like I was inducting him into knighthood. I pressed his shoulders down with my hands, forcing him to stay seated. His black felt hat blocked his face from mine, and I quickly snuck a peck on his lips. The sneak attack left him as surprised as I was. His cheeks flushed, bright enough red to see beyond the shadows of his new brim, and I giggled in triumph.

Today was my day.

"Look at you, cowboy!" Mom hooted. Her voice added to the red-hot coals in Gabe's cheeks.

"Thanks," he answered sheepishly. He turned to me in embarrassment, begging me to take it off with his green eyes.

"She means it, you look good!" I cheered him on and patted his back. I threw a pair of spurs from the closet at him. "Use them with caution." The horse he would be riding didn't need spurs; he would carry him wherever we went. But Gabe needed the spurs. He needed to look the part, and I did enjoy the boyish excitement radiating from him.

Three horses waited by the barn, their fuzzy winter hair starting to fall off in clumps. Their noses still fogged the cool spring morning, but I knew we would probably all be sweating within a few hours.

Two black pistols lay nestled in the bottom of a duffle bag

full of clothes. Angie pulled one out and checked that the magazine was full.

No hammer, just pull the trigger.

"Don't worry, I remember us coming out here to shoot tin cans a few summers ago. Use your instincts, sister." Angie smiled as she placed the cold metal in my hand. The grip of the 9mm fit nicely.

"This is a little more powerful than the .22 revolvers we shot, but I think I can handle it," I answered as she handed me a breast holster. She had never called me sister before, and I held on to the label for a few seconds before heading out the door. Her brown contacts glowed bright when I met her gaze. We mirrored each other's tight-lipped smiles. We were both nervous.

"Be careful out there," Angie whispered into my ear as she helped me secure the holster over my button-down shirt. Our fates were held in the sand of an hourglass, and each grain that fell added to the weight of our situation. It was one we had little control over. The events to come would make us more than friends or even battle associates—we *were* sisters.

We arrived at our starting point. The dilapidated windmill creaked, filling the silence after we killed the engine. Gabe stood in the way of the trailer gate. The horses clomped across the floor, startling him when they hopped onto the ground. His fear didn't match the pistol that hid in the back of his jeans. It didn't fit with his thick beard or his pectoral muscles, which were slightly peaked under the white fabric of his pearl snap shirt. But, nonetheless, it was there.

"We're just going to gather this pasture. Once we get them in there, we'll sort the pairs off from the rest of the herd." Dad spoke softly as the babies started to find their moms. "Gabe, this is your ride." The old, seasoned gelding was small in stature, and when Dad exchanged the reins with Gabe, there was a pause.

"How come she's riding the biggest horse?" Gabe scoffed.

"So, you're a size queen?" I laughed as I swung my leg over Scooby. Little did he know that Scooby was a freakin' spaz and with one wrong move, he would send his ass flying. Dad put him on Fred. He was the equivalent to the worn-down pony they take to birthday parties. Not even a screaming kid could make him buck.

"Well, I'm going to head to the far corner; you guys start pushing the girls to the sorting pens. I'll meet up with you there." Dad's voice carried as he trotted away. Gabe looked boyish again, standing there with the reins in one hand and his other arm hanging to the side.

"I can't get you on him!" I pointed at the stirrup. "You've gotten on a bike before? Same principle." I enjoyed bossing him around. The cattle had already started to gather at the sight of the horses. The mothers yelled when their babies didn't gather at their sides. The leather reins rested easy in my hands, and I didn't need much tension to guide Scooby. My nervous system seemed to regulate when I found home again in the saddle. I swiveled my head, looking around for my new intern.

"I've never seen you like this before." Gabe's voice stopped my head mid-turn.

"Like what?" I turned to face the moving cattle. I shushed them as we pointed our horses toward the sorting pens. It was an old set of corrals in the middle of three pastures, a great place to sort the pairs from the rest of the herd.

"Ever since we've been here, you haven't been drinking, popping Xanax, or . . ." He trailed off. "You haven't been flying off the handle at everyone," he finished. His posture made me uncomfortable. He slouched in the saddle with his large body hunched over the saddle horn, making him flop against the horse.

"Yeah, well I hope you're better in bed than you are at riding that horse." I confronted his observations with my own. He held his reins a little higher, looking around at his legs to see what he was doing wrong. It wasn't his fault, but it was strange to see him finally struggling at something.

"I feel normal when I'm here. And, believe it or not, I fit in with aliens and CIA agents better than I do the rest of society." Hooves and squeaking saddles created a soothing rhythm. It made me uncomfortable to talk about the person I'd been before all of this. For the first time, I saw my actions and self-destructive ways and their effect on others with clear eyes.

"We all just want to see you happy, Jess. We've had to stand by for so long watching you suffer. I think we just feel like we all owe it to you. There's no such thing as normal anymore, but if we can keep you from some of the drama, we're going to." He leaned over, trying to find my eyes. A tear hit my horse's neck, soaking into a strand of his mane.

"Jess?" Gabe coaxed, almost falling off his horse.

"I know. Just know that my entire life has been a lie. Keeping things from me only lengthens your noses." I mimed an invisible Pinocchio nose in an attempt to lighten the mood. "The secrets you all kept weren't saving me. They were killing me."

I finally made eye contact, but something pulled my focus from him almost immediately when I noticed the hooves of our beefy companions had suddenly become louder. My head snapped forward, and I saw that Scooby's ears were perked. His skin was trembling, and the herd ran in all different directions. My hands hardened around the reins, gripping them in preparation, and Gabe's horse started spinning in confusion. I couldn't see why the animals were panicking.

When I turned around, I looked to the far corner of the pasture where Dad was. He was on top of the hill waving his arms, frantically pointing forward. One arm held the reins to his horse while the other flailed in a panic. His sorrel mare's feet were choppy, closing the distance between us faster than I'd ever seen before. When Dad cleared the hill, Scooby and Fred pulled against our hold on their reins.

A bullet-shaped vehicle followed him over the hill. Its distance above the ground revealed it had no wheels. Drone-like propellers pushed it closer and closer to us. Pieces of vegetation flew through the air as shots were fired around Dad.

"Give him his head!" I screamed at Gabe. My spurs dug into Scooby, signaling him to turn it on. "Loosen your grip, damnit!" Gabe's horse started to rare against him. When he understood my direction, Fred lunged forward, almost throwing Gabe off the back of the saddle. Dad reached us and the three of our horses met.

"Spread out!" I commanded the men on either side of me. Scooby's long legs stretched and we pulled ahead of Dad and Gabe. I stood up in the saddle, leaning forward to give him room to run. I shut out the rest of the world, and all I could see was the movement of his mane. His black hair wisped as we picked up speed.

I dared myself to look back, knowing we had no chance of escaping the machines. As we continued moving forward, I twisted my neck to glance at my fate. A horse screeched, and I saw hooves and boots flying through the air, landing and rolling in the dirt.

"Dad!"

The ship closed in, aiming for another shot. My horse slowed, still moving farther and farther away. Half a second passed, and before the shot was fired, the ship exploded. The bullet ship was no match for the massive blimp that trailed behind it. I dug my heels into my stirrups and pulled the reins to stop. Scooby skidded to a halt, and the momentum almost split my body in half.

The Veritans are here.

CHAPTER

THIRTY-TWO

THE BLACK MACY'S THANKSGIVING DAY PARADE BALLOON WAS NOT plastic. Shiny metal glinted bright in the sun. It hovered, covering a football field length of the pasture near where Dad had gone down. I contemplated whether to run or move toward the mangled mess of horse and human. Legs extended as the ship made its way down to the ground. Hydraulics whined as the mechanical feet gripped the pasture, and I loped hastily to Dad.

His horse's leg was broken. They had tripped.

Checklists materialized in my brain, and I began to catalogue the importance of tasks and assessment of injuries. Dad became my patient, reminding me of the part of medical school I was good at. Green grass and pasture blurred around me, the volume muted. Memories of clinical hours in the ER and trauma floor resurfaced. Car wrecks on the interstate had brought many patients similar to the one before me. The vehicle was different, though.

Dad screamed as the weight of his horse crushed his body. He was trapped. I formed a small lasso and swung, aiming for the horse's neck. When it caught, I looped my slack around the saddle horn. Scooby heaved against the tension of the rope. Dad's horse flopped like a fish out of water, beating a scream out of Dad.

Tap, jingle. Tap, jingle. My spurs coaxed my tow truck of a horse to keep walking forward. With a few lunges, we dragged the horse forward, uncovering Dad's horse-blanketed body. Once I revealed the damage, my eyes darted around looking for help. Gabe was nowhere to be found. Mom and Angie were at the house.

No professionals there to help me.

Dad screamed, reaching for his leg. His fibula and tibia seemed to be broken. My belt made a quick tourniquet above the knee. Blood had started leaking from the wound where the weight of the horse was keeping pressure on it. In the hospital we would be asking for meds, pumping morphine . . .

I had nothing.

Dad's screams were muffled by my focus. The anatomy, the physiology, it all screamed louder. My focus was on my training, because in this moment, I was no longer Jessica. I was Dr. Gray.

"Someone needs to call your mom," Dad said through gritted teeth. He was a tough son of a bitch, and I realized any of my other patients would have passed out from the pain by now. His face was covered in blood and scrapes from hitting the shrubs of sage brush on his way down to the ground.

"Dad, I love you, but shut your mouth and let me work. Angie and Mom are probably the reason you aren't dead right now. See the big ship? Why don't you look over there for a second." I'd tricked him, and the minute he saw the ship, I yanked on his leg, setting the bones back to where they should be. That was when he finally blacked out.

A group of suited aliens marched out of the ship, circling

around me and barking instructions in another language. I stepped away as they hooked up IVs and performed more paramedic treatment.

These were the good guys.

Their gray blue skin varied in shade from one individual to the next. They were oddly similar to humans, yet wildly different. The language that passed between them was rough, glottal. Harsh throat noises emphasized the spaces between the words that bounced around among the Veritans. Their teamwork was impeccable, and I glimpsed the same medical supplies that I would have asked for. They had come prepared; they knew they might need them.

They knew we were in danger.

Their aquatic looking bodies moved around me, oblivious to the fact that I was there. The adrenaline dump was wearing off and the shock of the situation set in. I sat in the dirt, letting the chaos continue without question. The more control I lost, the easier it was to accept.

Between the blur of people, I saw a figure walking forward, and when one of the Veritans bent down to put a gurney under Dad, I realized it was Gabe. He was on foot, no horse in hand. His hair was coated with dirt and his teeth seemed to be lined with mud. It looked as though his horse had stopped and his body hadn't stopped with it. He absolutely ate dirt.

"Your mother is on her way. I'm so sorry we didn't come sooner. This one flew right under our radar," a tall Veritan said in English. Her figure was majestic, with a long neck and head held high. She was older, pristine. Her voice was stern with authority.

The commander.

I could hear the Ram diesel coming down the two-track we'd ridden in on. Relief flooded through me, but I was too tired to speak. I stared forward, waiting for the right time to allow my mind back into the real world.

We were in deep shit now.

Bodies, bodies, bodies, human and foreign, bustled around me. There was little for me to do when our reinforcements took over Dad's medical care. He was in the middle of a pasture with medical grade supplies surrounding him. Authoritative voices fought for their place in conversation. I remembered the way it felt to be in the emergency room. Professionals acted on training, and certain commands moved them in unison.

The commander, Mom, and Gabe spoke in tones that worried me. There was a sense of urgency that made me realize our little fairy tale on the ranch was over. I watched them point their fingers and cross their arms, and at times I saw a pause in conversation.

Dad's rough face was relaxed. His arm lay in a sling as they wheeled him into the ship. The IV most likely dispersed pain meds through his shell-shocked blood vessels. He was going to be OK, for now.

"Hold on, where are you taking him?!" I snapped out of my shock. The commander was pulled from her conversation when my voice cracked.

"I have a surgeon aboard the ship who will work on your father's leg. We won't take the ship anywhere right now, but you may not see it after you leave. We will turn on our camouflage settings. Don't stress, child, you're safe now." She looked at me, waiting for my stance to come out of defense mode. Mom watched as well, waiting to see if she would need to intervene.

Before I could relax my shoulders and unflex my legs, a mangled creature rose from the scraps of metal that had just exploded. The commander's eyes widened at the sight of my fear. Memories of Luke's pixelated body flashed before my eyes as I took in the form of the Mendaxian in front of me. Their face was more lizard-like, the crimson red the most marked difference from the Veritans that surrounded me. The Mendaxian's legs and arms were gangly, reaching forward with each limping step they took.

Mom started running toward me, trying to stop me from pulling my gun. Before she could reach me, I fired a shot just to the left of the commander. I stepped forward, unloading my clip into the chest of the Mendaxian who'd just tried to kill my dad. They continued moving forward as each bullet jolted their body. When the commander finally realized I wasn't attempting to murder her, she found her own weapon. She pulled her own trigger on a long-barreled handgun. There was no place for bolt action or a magazine, but it was filled with something. Force exploded from the tip and enveloped our enemy in a flash of visible heat. Whatever was contained in the small tank of her firearm had just vaporized an entire physical body. What was once a living thing dissipated into a million specks of slime and bodily fluid.

"Nicely done, Jessica. You do take after your mother." The commander holstered her weapon, unbothered by the interaction that just took place.

The gun felt heavy in my hand, regardless of the empty clip. I used training that I had never used without supervision. I killed another being that was after me. I had killed many four-legged predators and herbivores that provided our family with food. But I had never killed something capable of pulling the gun on me. My oath as a health care provider was trumped by the urge to protect my family. I remembered how naturally the doctors I had shadowed for the last few years would deal with chaos. As I sat in the dirt, I didn't understand how this had become my life. From the looks of the commander after she blasted the evil creature to bits, it seemed like she had been a trained killer for quite a while now.

I had a bad feeling this would become normal for me too. My life here and my life in Denver had been training me to become who I was right now.

Mom found her way to my side, leaving the conversation with the others. She gently grabbed the hanging weapon from my white-knuckled hand.

"I think it's best we get you home. Angie and Gabe are going to handle the rest of this mess for the night, and we'll regroup tomorrow," she assured me without looking at me. It was weird how she knew how to interact with me. She knew she didn't need eye contact from me for me to hear her. She didn't pry or prod my blank eyes. She knew me. With that much distance and time, she still knew me better than anyone else.

"Dad is in good hands, but I'm sure you know that. Do you think you can handle driving the pickup and trailer back?" she asked. I had forgotten about the horses. They'd probably made their way down to the sorting pens when the ships landed.

"Yeah, I just have to handle Dad's horse." I nodded at the injured living vehicle. The mare was broken in more places than Dad, and her last breaths would be taken as a hero who'd carried him to safety when she didn't have to.

"I can have someone else do it, Jess. Just go get in the pickup so I can take you to Dad's rig." She tried to nudge me in the other direction. The horse was breathing shallow breaths, covered in blood and dirt where I had dragged her off of Dad. Her sweat still soaked her patchy hair, her muscles straining. She was an athlete, and a loyal one. I held my hand out and Mom handed me her pistol.

"You did good, girl." I patted her head, brushing my hand over her distressed eyes. I stood above her, aiming for a humane end. Closing my eyes, I wrapped my swollen finger around the trigger. The shot was loud, quieting the rest of the crowd. I pointed the gun down and shoved it into Mom's chest. If I'd had any tears left to cry, they would have fallen down my face, but the frog I knew so well thumped against my chest, unable to escape. I wanted him to, but my body had no energy to acknowledge him.

"Let's go," I barked, heaving myself into the lifted Ram pickup.

CHAPTER
THIRTY-THREE

THE BARN STILL SMELLED OF SWEET GRAIN FROM EARLIER AS I unsaddled the surviving horses. The fermented scent was pungent yet comforting. The shuffle of hooves and my boots on the concrete floor made the rest of the day ahead seem a little less overwhelming. Each saddle fit back in its respective spot on the storage racks in the barn, and when I removed the pads underneath, revealing the sweat from earlier, I was reminded of our near-death experience.

When I let the horses out of the barn, they found their way to the dirt, rolling their sweaty bodies around and kicking their feet in the air.

Maybe I should try that.

The floor didn't need swept, but I found a broom anyway. This was the first time I had been truly alone in months, and sweeping felt like therapy. It started with just sweeping the saddling area, but then I moved to the tack room. The rough poured concrete grabbed at the bristles of my broom. The feeling and the sound of the brushing slowly rocked me in a steady movement.

A jingling of metal and wood pulled me from my self-made lullaby and I perked my ears. I was a deer in a meadow, waiting for the next predator to come and scoop me up.

"You guys home?" I sheepishly squeaked. The bravery from earlier suddenly left my body. I was alone. The pen next door was a shelter where we kept cows and their babies on occasion. It was connected to the barn by another gate. Someone was trying to get in from the other side.

My boots tapped lightly as I crossed toward the barn entrance that connected me to where the intruder awaited. A hole in the bottom of the wooden door revealed a break in the light shining through. A shadow moved in front of the peephole. I looked through to see a small cottontail rabbit making its way to the corner where it found its nest of new babies. The tension in my shoulders fell to the floor.

It's just a fucking rabbit.

"Angela?" A low voice made the sour feeling beneath my rib cage fester.

"Who's there?!" I shouted. The only answer was silence. When I reached down for the loaded gun, all I found was my empty holster. The spaded shovel was the closest weapon I could find, and I held it like a baseball bat, ready to slam a Mendaxian over the head.

I kicked the door open and swung my shovel at a large figure about a foot taller than me. His crimson hand caught the splintered handle before I could crack him right in the skull.

"It's Luke. I'm Luke!" When I realized I wasn't going to physically defeat the new species that sat in front of me, I let go, unleashing a few splinters into my hand.

"FUCK! You aren't supposed to be here for two more days!" My fear quickly transformed into anger.

I can't get one second of peace anymore.

"Calm down, Earthling. Your panties seem to be wadded."

He sneered as he circled me in the pen. Arrogance radiated off his bald head. The afternoon sunlight came from the west as the sun made its way past noon, and the rays shone down on his skin, revealing a similar iridescence to Angie's. Except underneath it were layers of scaling armor, a deep crimson red like rusted metal.

"You are definitely Angie's brother." I postured myself toward him, snatching the shovel back out of his grip.

"Put it down." He rolled his glowing eyes, and I lifted it higher, ready to strike.

"How do I know I can trust you?" The head of the shovel stayed poised above my shoulder. With a swift movement, he swiped it from my hands and tossed it across the barn.

"Because I'm the reason you're not dead." He crossed his arms, making his pecs bulge forward through his tight black jumpsuit. "Mother dearest won't be happy with me, but what's new." The tone in his voice changed, and he leaned back, uncrossing his arms. His reptilian fangs flashed as he smiled, and I shuddered a little.

I'd just killed someone that looked so similar to him.

"Great," I answered.

"Sorry about the rough entrance. I'm kind of a fugitive on the loose. They have a price on my head. Burned the plant down on my way out." He shrugged his shoulders.

"I killed someone today." I tried matching his energy, and he was unfazed.

"First time?" As he moved closer, I studied his facial structure. Thicker protruding scales formed his eyebrows, and his high cheekbones were intimidating. "You'll get used to it, kid. Welcome to the rest of the galaxy." He walked past me and rubbed my shoulder. His large hand shook my body.

Kid?

From the way Angie spoke of him, he wasn't that much

older than us. My sarcasm slipped away, and I felt childish watching him walk away from me.

"Hey, where are you going?" I stumbled after him, almost missing the closing gate that swung toward me.

"I'm going to talk to the adults about how we're supposed to prevent a galactic war after what just happened. OK, Earthling?" He paused to wait for my response.

What a dick!

When I didn't answer, he kept walking, huffing on his way to the house. Tires rumbled over the cattle guard, and I jumped, still too skittish. I pranced to the house, realizing Luke was letting himself in. His build, boxy and muscular, took up the entire doorway.

My teeth cracked under the pressure of my anxiety. *Who does he think he is?* The dirt kicked up under my marching feet, my spine straightening on my way to meet him inside. I was ready to tell him off, but there was one problem.

He terrified me.

CHAPTER
THIRTY-FOUR

TOMORROW.

The meeting had been moved up a day because of Luke's loud entrance into the atmosphere.

Tomorrow we would have to face the CIA.

The door crashed down and jumbled footsteps and shouts came from the foyer as Luke and I sat awkwardly at the kitchen table. The argument between Mom, Angie, and Gabe stopped immediately when they saw Luke.

"Hi, Lucious. Thanks for pissing Mom off." Angie let the door slam behind her. As time went on, I was glad I didn't have a sibling. I also realized that my mommy issues weren't near as deep as Angie and Luke's. We had interracial turmoil here on Earth, but I had never seen intergalactic half-siblings. Was that even the term?

"Do you know how hard the commander and I have worked to achieve quiet airspace? Do you know how long we've studied the sky to get people here safely?" Mom started in on Luke. His fangs hid underneath a tight scaled lip. He was about to start laughing. "And you just come in like a bull in a

China closet. And you . . ." She looked straight at me. "You lied."

"How's it feel?" My nails clicking against the wooden table were the only sound in the room. Deep belly laughter rumbled out of the large Mendaxian who sat next to me, and everyone continued staring. My fingernail found a sticky piece of syrup on the table, picking it over and over until it was malleable enough to roll around. I kept my focus there until the laughter stopped.

"It wasn't all his fault. Our little friend from the Gibbons ranch ratted us out," Gabe interjected, breaking the awkward silence. "The CIA is now watching me too. I don't know how much trust they have in me at this point. In fact, I'm not sure if tomorrow's meeting will end in me getting whacked or fired." He walked past us, heading to the shower. The dirt from his pileup was still all over his face.

"So whose boyfriend is that? Yours or my sister's?" Luke leaned back in his chair to look at me. The blood left my lips and found my cheeks. My body was having such a visceral reaction to the embarrassment that it no longer felt the need to provide sustenance to my other extremities. "Is anyone going to talk about how dysfunctional this is? Also, where's grandpa?"

"Where is Dad?" I asked, realizing how inconsiderate I was. I hadn't even thought of that since I'd gotten home. I shot Luke a dirty look, making sure he knew that he could insult me, but not my dad.

"He's being taken care of in the commander's ship. He's in good hands; they have all the supplies we don't," Mom answered sheepishly. Her demeanor changed, and suddenly she wasn't so mad. She knew that we wouldn't have been able to get Luke here if we'd told her and the commander about our plan. He was literally our only chance at convincing the CIA that they couldn't go through with the deal.

Unfortunately, he was also the main reason our plan may not work.

"Why did you have to make a scene? You started a fire in the mines, stole a ship, and led them on a chase?! Always with the drama!" Angie piped in. The lecturing words were familiar. Familiar because she had had the same conversations with me for the last eight years.

Why did you have to make a scene, Jess?

She was good at babysitting because she'd had a lot of practice. Bickering, eyerolling, and the slamming of hands on the table flew around me like shards of glass. The noise cut at the outer barriers of my body, trying to find its way in. The image of Dad's body intertwined with his mangled horse flashed back and forth with memories of the Mendaxian blowing up into a million pieces. Luke's presence made my confidence falter. The way I'd missed the Gibbons' hired hand made it even worse. How had I confused his body language for nervousness? He had been undercover, listening for information to tattle on Gabe with. But Gabe's job was the least of my worries. Right now, his life was at risk.

Gabe entered the kitchen in his lounge clothes, a white T-shirt and baggy sweatpants. His hair was still spiked from the shower. The dirt no longer disguised his pale, worried face, and we all waited for direction from our CIA informant. What had he heard? Did they know what was up? Was the meeting we'd set up just a death sentence?

"My supervisor didn't mention anything other than some airspace activity they wanted to check out." Gabe was stoic. No emotion passed over his face as we all waited for more information. "They'll be here mid-morning to go over the sightings with me."

"Maybe they're telling the truth?" I added, knowing that was unlikely. Today's run-in would be hard to keep quiet, and our friendly neighbor had already spilled the beans that we were directing everyone to burn the contracts they'd received.

"I really thought the daughter of Agent Rodriguez would be a little smarter than that." Luke found a way to slip in more unneeded sarcasm.

"Would you shut the fuck up? Here I thought you were this great savior to the human race, and it turns out you're just a pretentious asshole!" The anger and angst from the day had reached its boiling point, bubbling uncontrollably out of my mouth.

"Oh, OK. That's more like what I expected from you," he responded without hesitation, waiting for my next comeback.

"Don't you give a shit about either of our planets? We're some of the only ones who haven't been taken over by these assholes. Do you want us all to be slaves?" As I continued, Luke's fangs unclenched and his mouth opened in rage.

"Why would I give a shit about either? I belong nowhere. And I *am* one of those assholes, in case you forgot." He held out his arms and put his body on display as he stood up out of the kitchen chair. His large stature was much less intimidating when he was sitting down. "I have nothing to lose here. The only reason I came is for my sister." He grabbed the chair and threw it across the room with one hand. Wooden pieces went flying, and a large dent formed in the wall from the impact. The entire room shuddered, and before I could react, Luke was gone.

"Well, there goes our last chance at saving the world. Nice job, Jess." Gabe held his head with both hands, pacing between the doorway of the kitchen and living room. Angie followed after her brother and I leaned forward, pressing my face to the table.

"If you had told me he was coming, all of this could have been avoided," Mom said. Her voice was back to commanding, and she ended her sentence with a nice tinge of "I told you so." She knew who Luke was, and so did Angie. But we had to have physical proof—living, breathing proof that he was a slave to the Mendaxian leaders. Pictures, stories, and all the other evidence we had meant nothing to them.

My eyes stayed closed, and the table was cool against my forehead. I ignored her even though I could feel her impatience when I didn't answer. Gabe's footsteps kept a steady rhythm back and forth on the floor. I could have just gone to sleep, zoned out and avoided the problem. But my phone buzzed against the table, making my forehead vibrate.

Trip.

"Hello?" I said, insinuating I didn't want to talk.

"Have y'all turned on the news? Fuel your vehicles and get out your ammo. I don't know what this is, but it isn't good." Trip wasn't making much sense. His twangy voice seemed more serious than usual. I fumbled with the remote with one hand while I held my cell phone to my ear.

Mendaxians flooded the screen. The footage showed ships similar to the one today landing in concrete jungles across the country—New York, Atlanta, San Diego, and Denver. Subtitles scrolled across the bottom of the television as the president spoke. "They mean us no harm. House our friends from Mendax, and in return we will have another Earth. A home away from home."

"Trip, I need you to do me a favor." I paused, and all I could hear was his breathing and the muffled television. "I can't explain everything right now. It's . . . It's a lot. But I need you all to be here tomorrow afternoon. All I can say is that it has to do with those crooked deals. Do you understand?"

"Yes, ma'am."

THIRTY-FIVE

WHEN I HUNG UP THE PHONE AND TURNED AROUND, GABE AND MOM were watching the screen behind me. They looked at me, then at each other. The two people who always knew what to do were lost.

"I don't think they care about being sneaky anymore." I threw the remote on the couch. Mom spoke into a silver device with a large antenna, communicating with the commander. The rough dialect that came out of her mouth cued me to leave the room. If I couldn't understand her, there was no point in listening. We were all probably going to die anyway.

The hot water ran out about halfway through my shower. It was probably a good thing because I could have stood there until my skin melted away from my muscles. The hot water grounded my dysregulated body. It kept me from wanting to run away.

I was proactive, adding lotion to my scalded skin as I sat at the side of my bed. My old basketball shorts and sports T-shirt relaxed my skin where my jeans had dug into it and my shirt had bunched from being tucked in. I wriggled my toes, reminding them they weren't in boots anymore. The fluffy comforter gave me a big hug as I tucked myself in before the most important day of my life. I stared at the ceiling praying that we would be able to pull this off. I prayed that my family reunion wouldn't be cut short.

The elephant in the room trumpeted around while everyone ignored him. Our only option would be to flee. Why we didn't run right now was beyond me. Gabe's job was long gone, unless he turned on us. What if he was the reason all of this was happening?

The intrusive thoughts swirled through the cortex of my brain, filtering their way in and out of my ears. They buzzed, they hummed, ringing the tiny bones in my ears over and over again. I was questioning the trust I'd built with the family around me. Who was really on my side? Dad? Mom was from another planet, a stranger. Angie, same situation. Gabe wasn't even a fucking doctor. He had been faking it all that time. Who did I believe? How did I know they weren't all lying to me to serve their own interests?

A light knock tapped against my door. The hug from my heavy blanket now felt suffocating. I had to put my mask back on. I couldn't even trust my own feelings.

"Jess, are you decent?" Gabe whispered from the other side of the door.

"That's a great question," I softly replied. He opened the door, letting it slowly creak shut behind him. He sat at my feet and rested his hand on my shin. "I am far from decent." I played around, always avoiding the situation at hand. His hand tightened around my ankle, the sensation a fine line between pain and comfort.

He was nervous.

"I just wanted to say thank you for accepting me into your home. I know we were always friends, but this is different. This is your home turf, and I finally feel like I know you." He looked down at the covers, avoiding eye contact. The conversation felt like goodbye, and I begged the bones in my ears to stop ringing. They wouldn't stop pounding against my eardrum with angst.

Focus.

"Yeah, Denver wasn't really my thing, as much as I wanted it to be. I wanted to be more than this place." I motioned around at the creaky old home.

"But what if you could just accept that you're all the places you've experienced? It's obvious med school wasn't a waste after today," he continued. "You're part of two different organizations fighting for the world's rights. I would say you're doing better than you think." His grip loosened.

That was hard for him to say. He didn't like talking about his feelings any more than I did.

"It mostly just solidified the idea that I'm a freakin' hot mess and trouble follows me," I said, deflecting his compliment.

"Don't do that." He finally looked at me. I met his gaze with an apologetic smirk and a one-armed shrug. Turning forward to face the old posters on my wall, he began to dissect each boy band and pop star, but the intensity in his eyes wasn't interest. Before I could interrupt him, he sat next to me. The bed groaned with the added weight.

"Remember the party at the speakeasy?" He raised his eyebrows and smiled.

"What about it?" I played dumb.

"Remember when you used your body to seduce me into leaking information?" He squeezed my thigh three times, letting his hand hover a second longer than usual. I stared at his smile, confused on where this was going. My palms suddenly felt sweaty again. Before, I'd escaped my feelings by drinking too much, cussing at people on the street, and passing out after popping anxiety meds. Since I'd been home, there were no escapes, and it was equally liberating and terrifying.

"That took a slight buzz and anger to pull off." I placed my hand over the one he still had on the inside of my leg. Sweat formed between our hands, reminding me that clammy was my middle name.

"So, what would impending doom and exhaustion do for you?" With his other hand, he took hold of my face and waited for me to close the final ten percent of space between our lips.

Over eight years of school, my drunken nights had always made it look like I was the class slut. I'd flirted my way through conversations and even gone home with guys a few times. The truth was that I'd only had sex with my high school loser of a boyfriend, and after that a few casual daters. I spent a lot of time questioning who I was, and letting people in wasn't my strong suit. This moment with Gabe felt like losing my virginity all over again.

When our bodies found each other this time, it was with fear. Fear that after tonight, there would be no more chance of an us. Fear that sex, love, and emotion wouldn't be part of our lives anymore. Fear that this would be our last night together.

Every movement brought memories of our time together. His hand on my waist in the club, the smell of cheap booze at the college party, his nervous look when he hopped on his horse for the first time today.

There was no humming or buzzing in my head anymore. The bees of worry and angst seemed to have left the building.

If the world did end after tomorrow, I would be fine with going out like this.

CHAPTER
THIRTY-SIX

TODAY.

Gabe's arm and leg trapped me in the spooning position. When I heard Mom's voice in the kitchen, I extended my arm as far as I could to reach my phone. It was only four in the morning. They spoke softly in Angie's native tongue. Angie was back, but I didn't hear Luke.

It took all my strength to remove the deadweight off my body and stumble into the kitchen.

"Where's Luke?" My voice wasn't fully awake yet, and neither was the rest of my body. My right eye was still crusted shut, and my hair was matted to my face. Angie and Mom wore the same look of curiosity and amusement. "What?" I quickly patted down my hair and rubbed the sleep from my eyes. They kept staring, putting me under a spotlight.

"Luke's gone. His ship is gone, and the commander doesn't have eyes on him." Mom looked down at my feet. I realized my underwear were wrapped around my ankle, and the large T-shirt I wore was barely covering me.

"Rough night?" Angie teased. She had taken her contacts

201

out and her fluorescent eyes didn't complement her human skin. Embarrassed, I bent over to pull up my underwear just as Gabe walked up behind me. I felt his hands on my waist. He'd grabbed me out of surprise, not aware in his half-asleep stumbling.

"I am so sorry!" he shouted, jumping back.

"Well don't act like you haven't seen it before! Jesus Christ!" My face was red hot, the fumes of anger and embarrassment evaporating through my ears. Angie's giggles filled the room, but Mom's stare silenced her immediately. Until they both dissolved into laughter, that is.

"Alright, alright. Jess and Gabe had sex, the world is ending. HA. HA. HA." I waved my hands around, mocking Mom and Angie. Once their giggles faded, we all sat around the table for a meeting of the minds. We all scanned the circle, deciding who would talk first. No one wanted to volunteer.

Luke was half Mendaxian. He looked like the enemy, but I still believed his heart was in the right place. We needed him, and I'd ruined it.

"My supervisors will be here in a few hours," Gabe said, breaking the silence.

"And that's all the information you have?" Mom pressed harder, still not trusting him completely. I suddenly felt gross. A part of me wondered if he was lying. What if I'd just slept with the enemy? He was supposed to be on our side, but what if it was all part of his game?

Intrusive thoughts, intrusive thoughts, intrusive thoughts.

Once I pushed the returning buzz out of my brain again, I suddenly felt anger toward Mom. She and the commander claimed to have all of these ideas, these plans to save people. But when I thought about it, it was surprising that they hadn't made any progress over the last twenty years. Luke was a loose cannon, but he was making moves. They were too busy playing nice, keeping the peace, and protecting themselves. The people below them were the ones who suffered.

"He's telling the truth. I checked his phone last night and this morning," Angie defended him before Mom could dig further. Everyone chewed on the problem, swishing it around in their mouths to figure out how we would swallow the truth. The CIA may not have said anything yet, but that didn't mean they didn't know what had happened yesterday.

"I think I should go back, maybe try to explain what's going on," Gabe blurted out.

"Absolutely not. You're staying right where I can see you," Ang answered before Mom could say the same thing. We were at a stalemate, but it was only a matter of time before shit hit the fan. Our Hallmark fairy tale was coming to an end.

"I think you should just show them what happened. Why not? We didn't technically do anything wrong. Play dumb. Pretend we had no idea Luke or the commander were here." When there was no response, I continued. "Let's just show them the weird alien guy all blown to smithereens. Say we found it while we were moving cows. Lead them in a different direction, buy us some time!"

"It's not a bad idea," Mom said, looking thoughtful. "Bringing them out here also may make them more comfortable with you, Gabe—build their trust even more. If they think they can trust you and Jessica, they won't be as hard-pressed to monitor us. The Mendaxians are here, but they shouldn't be using military force. I don't believe that was part of the deal. They're supposed to be 'peaceful.' The chaos going on right now could help our case when we try to convince them they definitely aren't the good guys they portray themselves to be." Mom pushed her chair out from the kitchen table.

"I'll work on a script for Gabe to use when they get here. No funny business or improv. Got it?" Angie looked at Gabe, waiting for a nod of approval.

"Meet in here in an hour." Mom turned her back to us to start a pot of coffee. She had the right idea. "Get yourself decent, Jessica," she added before I could exit the kitchen into the living room. I kept my face down, watching my feet squish into the old shag carpet. The sink and the toilet ran as everyone prepared for the day of reckoning. Maybe if the CIA saw the Mendaxians creating havoc where they weren't supposed to, we could make moves to fight against them. But part of me felt like it was too late. We were in too deep, and these space guns and slave-driven armies were larger than we were ready for. The government had absolutely screwed us.

After throwing on some clothes, I made my way into the kitchen to meet Mom with the fresh percolated coffee. Gabe and Angie were upstairs going over what to tell his supervisors when they got here.

"There's a possibility we'll have to flee," Mom said under her breath, startling me. She held her coffee and stood beside me as I poured my own. Her proximity stunned me, and I slowly set the coffee pot back on the stove. "If this goes south, I can get us out of here quick, but I want you to know now . . . He can't come with us." Both of us stayed facing the stove, not making eye contact.

I nodded, knowing that it wasn't an if, it was a when.

And I would have to leave Gabe behind.

THIRTY-SEVEN

Any minute now.

Our stomachs had nothing in them but caffeine and worry. We looked like Pac-Men in the kitchen, pacing back and forth, running into dead ends, and turning around. All of us were running from the inevitable as we waited for the agents to arrive.

Gabe was going to leave out the details. He was doing his job, exactly as they had asked him. But it was a perfect chance for us to point out that the Mendaxians were not being very peaceful. If there was any way at all to keep this "low-key," we were going to try. After draining two pots of coffee, Gabe, Angie, and I all turned at the sound of a vehicle rumbling over the cattle guard. It was the closest thing we had to a doorbell, and it gave us a little time to scurry into our set places. Mom and Angie would be above us looking down from the upstairs window. They had the commander on standby, waiting behind the house in the west pasture. If we had to run, Dad was going with us.

Through the window I watched one black sedan make its

way into our driveway. My hands jittered from the caffeine, and the coffee sloshed around in my stomach. At least it was only a few agents. The lack of warm bodies and armored cars signaled to me that they didn't know the full story. They were too preoccupied with their friends taking over major cities to worry about us. The car rolled to a stop, its exterior covered in soot collected on fifteen miles of dirt roads. From what I could see, there were two agents sitting in the front seat of the vehicle: a man and a woman. The doors opened in tandem. Before I could move to open the door, Gabe grabbed my hand, intertwining our fingers and giving me a good squeeze.

"Stick to the script." I squeezed his hand back.

"Got it," he answered, giving one last squeeze before he beat me to the door. The screen door banged behind us, and I tried to disguise my flinch. Then the two car doors slammed within milliseconds of each other, mimicking the gunshots I'd fired the day before. My legs were gelatin, and my heart was lead. This didn't feel right.

"Agent Harris, this had better be good. I didn't exactly want to spend my Sunday in bumfuck Egypt," the tall bald man huffed. I remembered him from the basement dungeon where I first found out Gabe was an agent. Now that the shock had worn off, I noticed his stature made Gabe look small. His shoulders almost tore his suit jacket when he put his arm out for a handshake. His partner, a woman, followed behind him. She was new. She seemed to be about my age, her straight face trying to camouflage her nervousness. My guess was that she was sent to shadow the wannabe Rock Johnson who was trying to intimidate us with his meathead muscles.

"Agent Smith, I just wanted to discuss some activity we saw over the weekend. I figured an in-person meeting was appropriate." Gabe waited for the meathead to nod before he continued on. "Two different foreign life-forms have been making their way down to Earth for a while now. I know that because Agent Rodriguez is on American soil. Our assumptions were right, and she is still alive," Gabe finished his thought, going completely off script. My eyes widened with surprise, and I had to hold myself back from darting around to alert Mom and Angie. Agent Smith's face contorted, his nostrils flaring as he turned his gaze on me.

This information sparked something in the bald man's eyes. Confusion, anger, and a loss of control pulled at the muscles of his face. It had surprised him. My legs locked as he scanned from Gabe back to me several times before answering.

"What do you mean she's on American soil? You've known this and didn't say anything?" His voice boomed as if he held a megaphone. His new partner flinched with surprise; she was clearly not anticipating this either.

"She touched down for one night and told us some very disturbing things. I've been trying to sift through her intel to make sure I had my facts straight. I didn't want to believe it, but yesterday we were attacked by a Mendaxian." Gabe rushed through his sentence before Agent Smith could get any redder. Angie and Mom had obviously done a good job covering their tracks and hiding any communications from the CIA.

"That's impossible. We would have seen. Either you start making sense, or we're going to talk about suspension," Agent Smith barked, getting more and more confused. If his employees weren't doing their job, that meant he was also in trouble.

"How long have you known about the deal we made with Mendax?" Gabe asked, barely opening his mouth.

"Oh, Nathan. You think you're so smart, but you've always wanted to be a hero. When are you going to learn that doesn't get you to the top? Following orders and doing what you're told is the only way this is going to work, and it looks like you completely fucked that up." The agent's tone turned sarcastic; he was gaslighting us, turning the situation into something that wasn't that serious.

"Answer the question," I said through gritted teeth before Gabe had the chance to continue.

"You silly little children. The world is ending! We've been sucking the Earth dry for the last 250 years, and Mendax is our only chance at starting over. If you were smart, you wouldn't have meddled and kept your mouths shut. You were some of the select few that would be relocated. You and your little girl-friend could have lived happily ever after." The agent reached for his gun. "The election is going to be our last year here, and after that we get a free ride out of here while the rest of the world burns."

They knew. They knew the whole time. They didn't care about losing Earth.

The female agent's eyes flashed to the upstairs window, and before Gabe could get his gun from his holster, a shot rang out. Brain matter and blood exploded. The headless suit fell, bending at the knees and tumbling to the ground. The body collapsed, revealing his murderer.

Luke.

His swagger radiated as he holstered his space gun, much smaller than the one his mother used. Large, swift steps brought him closer to the body.

"He was getting on my nerves." He kicked the lifeless mannequin. I should have been horrified, but all I could think was, *Fucking finally*. The balls this guy had, if Mendaxians even had balls. Regardless, finally, someone was fighting back.

"Don't shoot, don't shoot. I didn't know!" The other agent held her hands up in surrender. But before we could make our next move, another shot fired from above. Her body fell next to her partner's.

"FUCK!" Gabe screamed. I leaned against the tree in our front yard and heaved. There was no food in my stomach for me to throw up. Angie busted through the screen door.

"What the fuck were you thinking?!" Gabe fell to his knees, hands grabbing at locks of his hair in angst.

"We can't trust them! For all I know, you're in on it too!" Mom pointed her gun at Luke's head.

"Stop! Don't do this!" I pleaded. The silence was broken by the coughing of the dying agent.

"She didn't deserve to die!" Gabe lunged forward with his pistol, closing the distance between him and Mom. Before anyone could shoot, I put myself between them.

"MOVE!" Mom screamed.

I lowered my voice, trying to ignore the convulsing body that lay in the dirt. "If he knew about this, then why didn't he kill you when he had the chance?" The low tones of my voice echoed through the driveway. The burning fire that fueled Mom seemed to lower to a flicker. Her brown eyes smoldered, looking through me as I tried to make sense of her irrationality.

"I've got some bodies to hide. If you guys want to kill each other and leave me for dead, then go ahead and do it." I stormed off toward the tractor. After a few turns and whines, it puffed out black smoke from the top. The hydraulics lifted as I pushed the lever and finessed the bucket so I could move forward. Everyone watched in awe as I prepared to bury the bodies. "Oh, and I told the neighbors to come help us fight the government and the Mendaxians. So don't shoot them if they show up on our doorstep. And you, what the fuck is wrong with you?" I shot a glare at Luke.

"I couldn't pass up the entertainment. This is much more fun than working in the fiery gates of hell on Mendax." Luke shrugged. I was mad at him, but he was the only one who said what he meant. The steam, the smoke, and the red embers that had formed the background of his pixelated call reminded me of where he had been. He was the only one living in the mess that the Mendaxians had caused. And for that, he got a pass.

I went to say something back, but my energy was elsewhere. I had zero fucks to give at this point, and I didn't have time to sit and argue. We had a world to save.

CHAPTER
THIRTY-EIGHT

THE BODIES SCRAPED OFF THE GROUND, THEIR FLESH STILL FLEXIBLE, which was making it hard to get them into the bucket of the tractor. They flopped over every time I slightly touched them with the metal teeth of my machine. I tried not to disturb the dirt so we could cover up our double homicide.

"Why do you bother?" Luke said from below the cab of the tractor. His stature made his proximity to the window closer than I would have liked. He stared with glowing eyes, and he didn't seem to care if it bothered me or not. I wasn't sure if it was a lack of self-awareness or his outright arrogance that kept him from catching on to social cues. "Earth's on its way out anyway; no sense in wasting your last hours burying scum." He talked like I wanted to—unmasked, unruly, and truthful. Something I hadn't seen since this mess started.

As soon as I started to feel, I flipped my switch back to numb. Feeling made it too difficult. Luke wasn't used to being ignored, and I could feel his frustration when I continued loading the bodies in the tractor. The bald man hadn't necessarily deserved to die, but he was going to kill us anyway. His partner . . . Now that made me shiver. That could have been Gabe.

Regardless of what had just happened, we were in this alone. The government was never going to help us. They had no problem watching us all get left behind to die. Luke was right. What was the point of all of this?

Gabe had already had a few tantrums, throwing random objects and screaming into his hands. For the last half hour or so, he'd gone from raging to pacing in silence. Angie was inside keeping an eye on the computer monitors, waiting for Mom to formulate a plan. We kept communications discreet because as of now, no one knew of the dead alien or the dead agents.

Along with a little gravel, I successfully scooped up both bodies, shifting the stick in front of me to lift the bucket so I could move forward. I didn't even ask what anyone else was going to do, because this seemed like the most pressing matter. I didn't have the time or the patience to deal with Gabe's hissy fits or Luke's sarcasm. Mom and Angie typed away on their computers. It made it easier to avoid the problems that seemed to be arising at a rapid rate.

I didn't have time to dig a hole, and I knew of a pond not too far in the pasture behind the house. It wasn't ideal, but it would keep the bodies underwater while we figured out what to do next. Part of me was scared by what was happening, but the other part of me felt like there was nothing else to lose. The people in charge—the people we were supposed to trust— were ready to make us slaves to another planet. They were ready to work us until there was nothing left on our own planet. Then we would just wither away, dying a slow death of starvation and dehydration, and Earth would become a barren wasteland.

Besides the officials in charge of the United States, the five of us were the only ones who knew this information. Who knew what deals they had with other nations. The rest of the world had no clue what was coming for them. In four short years, there would be nothing left. The title I had so badly wanted became a distant memory. Doctor, Jessica, cowgirl . . . I was just one tiny speck on a planet coming to an end.

Tears ran down my face as I neared the old dam. The chains I'd grabbed before I left weighed me down as I made my way down the metal steps. I wrapped each of their legs with heavy metal. Dad had used these chains to pull vehicles around or to pull posts out of the ground. When I got back in the tractor, I lifted the bucket high, dangling it over the deepest part of the pond. With a loud *plop*, *plop*, both bodies splashed into the murky water. I laughed at the number of clues I'd left behind. Tracks led straight to where I'd dumped the bodies. The water wasn't terribly high, so it wouldn't take much to uncover the soaking corpses. Luke was right. This was all pointless.

We only had a few hours before agents from headquarters would try to contact Agent Smith. The question was, where would we go? What would Gabe do when we fled to Veritan?

I took my time making my way back to the house with the tractor in low gear. I figured the longer I took, the more time it gave everyone else to figure out what the fuck we were going to do. Maybe they had cleaned up the blood and dirt in the front yard. Maybe they had figured out what to do with their car?

Again, the least of our worries, Jess.

The popping of the tractor engine and the bouncing of the torn-up foam seat kept the thoughts away for the rest of the drive home. In our world of fight or flight, I was definitely ready to fly.

CHAPTER
THIRTY-NINE

I CRESTED THE HILL TO SEE A ROW OF PICKUPS AND TRAILERS LINING the driveway. Pearl snap shirts, worn jeans, shotguns, rifles, cowboys, cowgirls, farmers, and many many boots stood beside their boxy, dated vehicles.

They were waiting for me.

Trip spoke with Angie, Mom, and Gabe. Hands motioned in the air. Then Mom looked back to see me getting closer to the driveway. Luke was nowhere in sight. Thank God.

I played out a scene in my head as I got closer to the group of people. I thought maybe everything was OK. Maybe, just maybe, this had all been a dream. But when I climbed down from the tractor, I was met with disgusted eyes. My cheery face obviously did not match the tone that they had been ruminating in for the past hour or so.

"The young one said something to headquarters before she went down. I'm sure they tried to make contact again, but when no one replied . . ." Mom words flipped my smile into a frown.

"She must have had an earpiece in. I didn't even think to

check before you took them to the lake," Gabe pleaded. He was still upset, dwelling on the murder. He didn't like losing control, and although I wanted to treat him like he'd treated me, I kept my mouth shut. Suddenly, now that things weren't going as everyone had planned, it seemed like I wasn't such a drama queen. This shit was scary, and the magnitude of the situation was coming to a head.

I assumed we had thirty minutes or so until several black cars that looked just like the one Gabe had hidden would come barreling down our road. The murdered agents' car was behind one of the boxcars from an old train we kept by the house for storage.

"So, we just wait like sitting ducks? Also, do we really want to play nice now that we know we're all going to die soon?" I snapped. The strategizing was stupid. Brute force and ignorance was what this was going to take, and I did not see what we had to lose. Why was everyone acting like being cautious mattered?

"Where's Dad?" I remembered he was still injured on the spaceship, wherever that was now.

"The spaceship is still in the pasture you just came from, but they're ready to come as backup. There's no time to call anyone else in. I have no idea if Mendax will be backing up the agents now. I have no idea what we're up against." Mom stayed calm. The eleven between her eyebrows grew deep. I no longer felt embarrassed about mine, because this woman meant business.

The group was silent.

"What you've seen on the television is true. Our government made a deal with another planet, the Mendaxians," Mom said, facing the other ranchers. "Unfortunately, as you probably already know, this wasn't a deal made for all of us. We'll all be enslaved soon if no one fights back. Angie is from Veritan, our ally. And right now, all I can tell you is we need your help. We don't know who's coming, and we all may die today. But this is a small battle that will be the start of an intergalactic war." I noticed Trip standing in the bloody dirt. The gravel and sand had clotted together the once pumping blood. They watched Mom speak, but traded whispers among themselves. The hum of low conversation between the country folk seemed anxious. They stared at me. I was covered in blood.

As Angie began to take off her disguise, all they could do was continue to stare. They really had no other choice than to believe us. Everyone listening fidgeted in worry but held on to their weapons. They were ready to fight. But they looked around, clearly wondering who it was they would be up against. I couldn't help but think they may just use their weapons on us if they didn't believe us. The feeling was relatable.

The commander's spaceship hovered over the hill, landing next to the house. The metal claws I'd seen a few days ago touched down in the grass. Their legs chameleoned, disappearing into the background.

"How do we know the CIA found out we murdered their agents?" I nudged the idea forward.

"Jess. Stop." Gabe's eyes were tired.

"We're going to die, aren't we?" I searched the eyes of my family. None of them would meet my gaze. I could tell they were grasping for courage, but they were met with adrenaline and fear. Mom walked closer to me, her eyes becoming soft.

"We might, but we're going to fight like hell." She brought her hand up to her mouth to whisper into a small speaker. The commander was ready.

"Where's Luke?" I asked. He seemed to have this uncanny ability to show up or disappear at the most inopportune times.

"He fled the scene after you left," Angie said, shrugging.

"He's always going to do what's best for him." Her voice cracked a little; she was clearly upset at the mess her brother had made. When she looked up at me, all the sarcasm and false hope fell from my face. The elasticity my skin once held was gone.

This was it.

The silence was broken by a rumble in the sky. A chopper propelled down and a voice spoke through an amplified megaphone.

"Put your weapons down on the ground in front of you. Walk away slowly and put your hands in the air."

Black armored vehicles crossed the cattle guard, and a few black sedans like we'd seen this morning followed. Gabe walked forward, leaving his weapon behind.

"What are you doing?" I hissed under my breath. The helicopter blades chopped the air, and my voice was lost in the abyss. Gabe took his badge out of his front pocket, slowly presenting it. He moved forward, looking for a chance to make peace out of the situation.

Don't be a hero.

"Agent Harris, stand down," one of the suited men yelled from behind his car door.

"All cooperation from this point forward will ensure your safety," the voice from the megaphone continued.

"Mendaxians are responsible for the murders of both agents," Gabe lied, holding his hands in the air in surrender. "This deal isn't what you thought it was. They are dangerous."

Stop! Stop now, Gabe.

Subconsciously, I moved forward to reach for him. Before I could lift my leg to take a step, Mom and Angie moved in front of me. Neighbors around me posted behind their own vehicles. The barrels of rifles poked through open cab windows. Gabe continued to walk forward.

The agents' pistols pointed toward us, their focus trained on Gabe. My eyes scanned, trying to find a hint of surrender from all parties involved. The chopper blades seemed to slow enough for me to see a sniper crouched in the opening of the hovering vehicle. He squeezed the trigger of his weapon, punching the primer of a single precision bullet.

Gabe fell to his knees. The ringing in my ears made me not only deaf, but also blind. I saw nothing but his limp body in the dirt where I'd just scooped up the dead agents. The space around him was black with seeping blood, and rage burned from my toes to my chest. The frog beat violently against my throat now, forcing out a gargled scream instead of tears.

Yellow, red, and orange sparks brightened the black hole that surrounded him, and I looked up. The helicopter was exploding before my eyes, and the suits all peered up at the fireworks show of destruction. Some of them dropped behind their car door shields. I was dazed, the explosion making it hard for me to understand what was going on.

The Veritan ship hovered above me, rippling into view as it removed its invisibility shields.

"We have to go! NOW!" Mom screamed at me through the vibrations of the spaceship. I ran from her words, making my way to Gabe's lifeless body. Four hands caught me before I could reach him.

"I just have to say goodbye!" I dug my feet into the ground in protest like a small child.

Metal clanged, and more shots flew in our direction.

The neighbors. They came through.

A cowboy hung out the window of his truck with a pump-action shotgun while his wife drove them through the group of black sedans. Precision shooters shot at bigger targets, closer targets. They could eradicate prairie dogs, small varmints, and coyotes at 500 yards. Today they shot distracted agents as pieces of helicopter debris fell from the sky.

Men on four-wheelers and women in feed trucks surrounded the ranch. We outnumbered them. We were going to win the battle.

But we'd lost Gabe.

"The Mendaxians will be here any minute!" Angie squeezed my arm, but my body was crazed with anger, heavy with the weight of loss. I wouldn't budge. They finally let me go. My instincts kicked in, and two of my fingers went straight to his neck as soon as I reached the body. There was so much noise, but I tried to remind myself that touch was a different sense.

What do you feel?

Nothing.

"I can't feel anything!" I gargled through another scream. They knew I wouldn't feel anything.

I used my strength to flip him onto his back. His head was bleeding. The wires in my mind tried to connect the dots as I searched for a bullet wound. My hand snagged on his shirt just above his heart.

"Jess, we have to go now!" Angie looked up at the sky. Mendaxian ships were coming from the west.

"Please help me!" I squatted underneath his shoulders, threading my hands under his armpits in an attempt to scoop him up. Angie and Mom ripped me away from him and yanked me toward the ship.

"We talked about this!" Mom screamed above the sound of the hovering ship. "He's gone!"

"What about everyone else?" I met Mom's eyes as I fumbled backward up the ramp.

"Don't worry—they don't want them. They want us." I watched as the ramp shut the bottom of the ship off from the world. G-force sank my stomach into my pelvis, taking me from standing to sitting.

Familiar clangs hit the sides of the vessel. Small indentions appeared in the metal as we all sat in the quiet basement of the moving ship.

"We can move to the main quarters now." Mom walked toward a door with a scanner. The ship was no longer swerving, allowing us to stand steady. She scanned her hand on the pad, and we began moving toward the opening.

I pretended we were entering the ER, completely ignoring the fact that we were airborne. I found myself replacing the foreigners' faces with familiar nurses and paramedics. So far, my ability to disassociate had kept me alive, and right now I needed it to keep me sane.

Upon entry, Veritans swarmed the control room, where screens surrounded us in a circular array of monitors. Red lights flashing all over indicated enemies were after us. The harsh language was echoing, and the sound waves swarmed my head. I closed my eyes until it stopped.

When I opened them again, all eyes were on me.

FORTY

"GABE. WAKE UP, KID!"

Pounding. The beat in my eardrums was loud, reverberating through my skull. I was alive.

Jess.

"The worst is over. We thought we lost you!" The voice became louder, and a large silhouette stood above me. Headlights shone behind him, not helping my eyes come into focus.

"Blink twice if you can hear me!" The voice was no longer muffled, and I raised my arm to shield the light that spilled from a running diesel engine.

"Where's Jess?" I asked, but my tender chest ached against the words.

What happened?

"Well, kid, I think you may have some explaining to do." Trip held out an arm, offering his calloused hand to me. Around us, the black cars were shot to pieces, holes decorating the doors that had acted as shields. The shiny metal shimmered as several pickups lit up the area. A few Mendaxians lay mangled in the dirt, their yellow fluid leaking into the place that had become my home. Trip waited for me to speak, but I couldn't.

The bullet had frayed my button-down shirt, and I quickly broke all my pearl snaps in one motion, revealing the bullet-proof vest that had kept me alive. But that didn't explain my horrible headache. My hair was matted from blood and a large bump formed on my forehead, while another protruded from the ground.

I'd knocked myself out on a rock. A fucking rock. I knocked myself out when I was needed the most. I'd failed everyone.

"Does anyone need medical attention?" I ignored the pain in my chest where the bullet made impact. I started frantically walking around, sifting through the bodies to find Jessica.

"Gabe, she's gone. I thought you were part of that plan," Trip said, speaking for the crowd of rural people that stood before me.

"Where are they?!" My voice broke. Angie, Agent Rodriguez, Chuck . . . Everyone was gone. The rock scuffed the bottom of my foot, fueling my rage. I kicked it loose, reached down, and chucked it across the driveway. The group of people continued watching, unfazed by the rage I'd unleashed. It looked like they had seen much worse in the last few hours.

"Hey, cowboy, let's all just chat. There are no injuries. That big ship that left with Jessica made a pretty big dent in these assholes. Then we came in with our ammo to clean them up." Trip stepped toward me. His shirt was buttoned crooked, and his belly peeked through the stained fabric. His arms were raised in surrender, and I veered away from him. "God damnit, kid, I know you've been through a lot, but we don't have time. Obviously if you look around, turn on the news, look at your phone, this is what's coming for us. And it seems that you and Jess knew. Why didn't you tell us?"

The betrayal on his face reminded me of Jessica when she'd

first found out. These were good people, and I was wrecking all of their lives with this bullshit.

"I work—I *used* to work for the United States government. Jessica's mom is an ex-agent who rebelled against plans I was unaware were in place. By the time I found out there were ill intentions, it was too late." I looked down at the divot in the ground where the rock had once been. The desperate eyes of the ranchers pulled my chin up, reminding me that I was still the only one aware of the details. I was the leader now.

The Mendaxians were slowly but surely invading the United States, and it was only a matter of time until other countries began to fall. Everyone had a rifle slung over their shoulders. Fear and determination fought each other on their faces, and everyone seemed ready for direction. They were cowboys, cowgirls, kiddos, farmers . . . but now they were soldiers.

We were in an intergalactic war.

About the Author

Kelcie Martin is an author from southern Colorado. A born and bred cowpoke and a fierce advocate for the neurodivergent community, Kelcie writes stories inspired by her rural upbringing and her passion for making others feel seen. She is currently raising twin boys who are on the spectrum and enjoys writing as a creative outlet. You can find her on Instagram and Facebook @cowpokeswhocry.